EDWARD'S DIARY

VOLUME I : THE PREQUEL

Written & Directed by

Will Brooks

First Edition

ISBN: 9798845815897

Illustrations by AllStral.

Edited by Lauren Brooks.

This story has been rated PG-13. Parents strongly cautioned.

Some material may be inappropriate for children under 13.

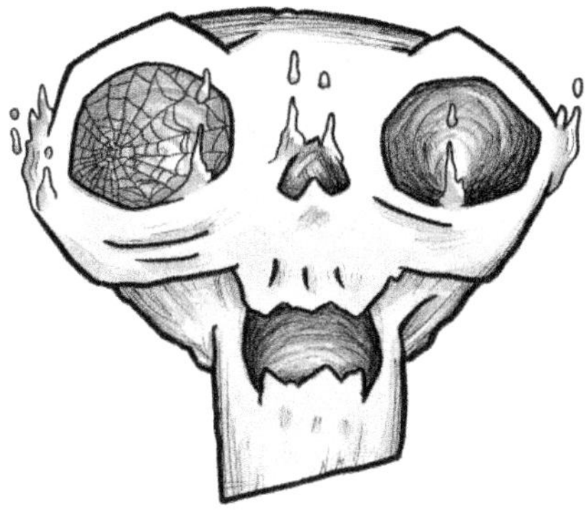

Scene Selection

PROLOGUE

Prologue

To whom it may concern,

It began in Spain. They called them 'Los Morados'. One minute we lived in a world without them. The next, they were here. Everywhere. Attempts of containment fell apart. Providing these things with help was never really an option. Plans to fight were aborted as quickly as they were conceived. The images viewed by millions online were too genuine not to be believed. Those that chose not to believe would find out the hard way that this situation, this nightmare was very real.

They simply called it 'The War'. There was no time for a group of writers to create a clever title for the newspapers. Entire countries were being destroyed, taken down like pawns on a chess board. Sacrificed to save others. Eventually even the Kings and Queens of the world all fell. Once all forms of communication ceased, tales of success from far away locations would provide people with false hope. Many traveled to find something that no longer existed. Although there was never any formal confirmation, 'The War' was lost. An entire species wiped out in a matter of months save for an unknown percentage. There are hundreds of fascinating stories belonging to these brave survivors. Tales of courage, strength, life, and death. Whispers of cures and new beginnings.

The story selected for these pages is the one of Edward. The reason for this is that even without 'The War', Edward's story was always going to be an interesting one. This is in no small part down to Edward's mother and the home she made for him. The stories that take place within those walls are quite unbelievable. Those that cannot suspend disbelief for fantasy and magic could never believe what went on in that house before 'The War'. If that event has taught us anything, it is that anything is possible.

What you are about to read are the scattered pages from Edward's diary that were found and carefully placed back in order.

Sincerely
The Quest Wizard

Fade up from black.

We open with a wide establishing shot of a beautiful old gothic mansion bathed in early morning sunlight. As the camera slowly zooms in on the building, we see that the windows have all been boarded up with planks of wood. The cracks in the walls start to become visible as we pull focus on the mysterious house.

We transition to a view of the inside of the property. Our protagonist is lying in bed with his eyes closed. The peaceful silence is interrupted by the sharp sound of an alarm clock performing its most essential function.

Opening Sequence

I open my eyes to the sound of the alarm clock, which for some reason is still working. The batteries inside just won't die, unlike everything else. I wonder why I still use it and whether anyone else out there still has any concept of time. The face reads eight o'clock, but in truth, I have no idea what the time is as there is nothing left to provide a basis for comparison. Why do I still use this?

I press the snooze button which once upon a time I loved the idea of. The dreamy sound designed to carry you effortlessly between asleep and awake ceases immediately, just like everything else. I'm still alive. The idea of facing another day brings the conflicting emotions it always does. Will today be my last? Probably not.

I admire the way you determine my daily preparation,
The way you deliver the pros and cons of any situation,
The way you present me with inspiration and relaxation,
The questions you raise never cease to amaze,
Do I really need a shower?
You always have the power to provide an extra half hour.

No matter how terrible I feel,
You recover me with secrets,
Like breakfast is an insignificant meal.

With just one press you ease my stress,
With one caress you extend my rest.
Your relaxed regime allows me to dream.
So, until I hear your final beep,
I shall just continue to sleep.

I love you, little button marked snooze,
You allow me to wake when I choose.

Exposition

My name is Edward.

For the first time in my life, I have started to write a diary. It's an odd time to start, given that I am probably the last person left alive in the world and no one will ever actually see these words. I guess I'm writing them for myself in an attempt to keep myself sane. Recently, I have found that to be quite a challenge. I am not a writer, so I may not be able to paint beautifully vivid images with my descriptions, use perfect grammar or even form satisfactory sentence structures, but I have an important story to tell, so I'm going to try and tell it.

It's been several years since The War started. At least I think it's been years. Years since the people disappeared and got replaced by those things out there. I was 14 when it started. I don't even know how old I am now. I have lost count of the days and years. I have managed to survive these last few years by staying inside my house. I live alone but at the same time, my house is filled with living things. This is something that I will have to explain...

My house is an old gothic building with three storeys and an impossible number of rooms. It's like one of those magic tents that looks tiny from the outside but when you walk in, you're presented with an acre of land. Although my house isn't small, it's certainly bigger on the inside. This is all part of the unexplainable magic that lives within these walls. Sadly, the magic that I speak of has no part to play in the ending of the world or the attempts to save it. That I know of.

I will try to drip feed the magic into the pages as hearing about it all at once could be quite unsettling and difficult to believe. These pages will contain diary entries of how my life in lockdown is going, as well as my account of the end of the world, poems, drawings and scripted scenes of other significant moments in my life.

If you are reading this, it means that I am not the last person left alive as I have feared for so long now.

Frank. If you're reading this, what have I told you about going through my things?

Backstory

The first thing I should do before I write about what happened is write about what happened before the beginning.

Believe it or not, the end of the world isn't the most interesting part of my story. It is a big scene, but not the main event. I won't bore you with the details of my complicated birth because it won't add anything to the plot. Instead, I will start by telling you about my mother and the home she made for me.

My mum was an inventor. Is an inventor? Was an inventor.

Now, I don't mean she just went on some sort of Dragon's Den TV show once, I mean she was a Dragon. Not literally, but she was a legendary mythical creature capable of magical feats that you would need to see to believe. I don't know if that's what everyone thinks of their mothers, but it's how I feel about mine.

Some of the things I'm going to write down here are going to sound unbelievable. In fact, most of it will, but every part of it is true. Sometimes I wish it wasn't, but it is.

Detailing everything mum achieved on these pages won't be possible, but I will try to include as much as I can. I guess the most important thing to tell you about would be her greatest achievement and her biggest mistake. Sadly, these are one and the same.

Here we go…

I'm going to start by telling you all about Frank.

The Sidekick

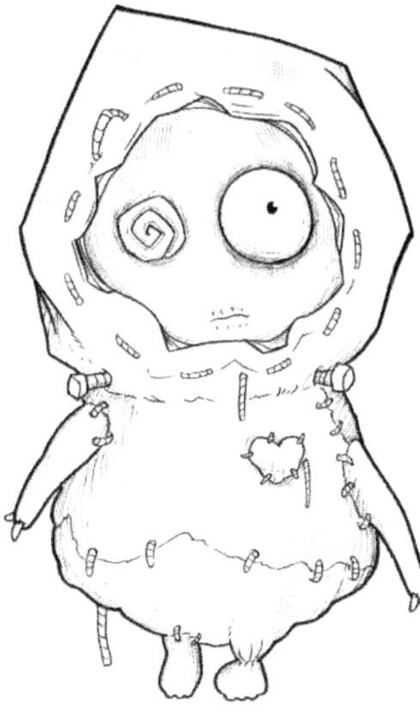

Ok, Frank is a living voodoo doll.

Bear with me.

My mum created him using my own DNA. Which means that I feel what he feels. He is a sentient being. He can walk, talk, and do all the things that humans can do. For the most part. He's capable of emotions. Very capable of emotions. Too capable.

It's a complicated situation, but before The War happened, my mum knew she was going to have to leave me, and she didn't want to leave me alone. She decided to create Frank to look after me while she was away. I don't think she knew just how long she was going to be away for. I also don't think she knew that it would actually be me that would end up looking after Frank. Or maybe she did.

Frank looks like a fat little pillowcase filled with soft old mushy fruit. He's got useless small legs which means he walks like a constipated penguin, and his arms are like half-filled sausages. He has been poorly stitched together, so he is constantly falling apart. His eyes are the worst; he has a creepy spiral button stitched on one side and a giant lidless eyeball on the other. He never blinks but he's also the most harmless creature you could ever meet, although when he's staring at you silently with those unblinking eyes, it's like something from a horror film.

Now, Frank is not an overly intelligent creature. He has a curious mind and likes to ask questions. He also likes to explore and test limitations, which, given the fact that I can physically feel what he feels, isn't great.

Once, when Frank wanted to find out how our toaster works, he thought it would be a great idea to explore the mechanics by putting his hand inside and pulling down the lever… in the middle of the night. That was not a great way to wake up. Also, his senses seem to be a lot duller than mine. He feels pain, but is able to withstand it for quite a while. This meant that he didn't actually take his hand out of the toaster until I came running into the room screaming in agony at 3'o clock in the morning.

You may think that when I first met Frank, I would have been shocked to see a living voodoo doll standing in front of me, drooling and staring, as his newly sewn on eyes were adjusting to seeing for the first time. But no. I grew up in this house where very strange things like Frank were an everyday occurrence. They still are, even now.

I never knew how mum created these things. She used to say something about using magical dragon scales to bring them to life, but I never believed her. It had to be something more scientific that no one could possibly understand. There isn't as much magic in the house as there was when my mum was here, but there is still a lot of strange and unexplainable things that happen.

I'll do my best to continue to explain them in these pages.

My relationship with Frank is a complicated one. He's sort of a mixture between an irritating puppy that won't leave you alone and an overly quizzical robot that you can't switch off. If I had to describe him in one word, it would be 'annoying'. If I had to explain him in two words, they would be 'very annoying'. You get the idea.

I chose to name him Frank because of the bolts that stick out of his neck. I have no real idea how my mum made him or what it is that actually gives him life. She never explained those types of things to me. I have always just accepted them. She never told me she was creating this doll for me, and she certainly never told me that she was using my DNA to help create him. I don't even know what that means. Did she take some of my hair when I was asleep, my blood, baby teeth?

Frank was my mum's final creation. That I know of anyway. He was the last thing she made before she left.

Before The War, my mum was always creating things. Her room was full of machines and computers. There were lots of cages with little creatures in them. Some that I recognised from the books at school, some that I didn't. I haven't been able to go into her room for a long time now. The door stays locked. She didn't like me going in there on my own and I've always held on to the hope that she would be coming back.

Frank is always desperate to try and get into mum's room. He can't help but want to explore. He's been everywhere else in the house, so naturally he is intrigued by the only room he's not allowed to enter. I have to constantly remind him that he's not supposed to go in there when I see him pathetically clawing at the door.

I would put Frank's intelligence level somewhere between a three-year-old child and a goldfish. He has a somewhat selective memory. There have never been any issues with him remembering where I hide the guitar that he's not allowed to touch as it belonged to my brother, but he seems to have a great deal of trouble remembering what happens when he tries to fly down the stairs.

As much as Frank annoys me, he keeps me company. Oddly, he gives me purpose because he depends on me. I haven't always felt this way about him. It's a strong word to use, but I really hated him when my mum left. I don't know why, probably because I didn't have anyone else to blame. I ignored him. I closed myself off. About a week after mum left, I locked myself in my room and starved myself until I became very sick. When I finally came out, Frank was stood outside my door waiting for me. He had been standing there for days.

Once you get passed his irritating personality and horrifying appearance, once you've answered a few thousand very similar questions, and once you've come to terms with the fact that you are occasionally going to wake up in the middle of the night in excruciating pain because he's learning what boiling water drunk straight out of the kettle tastes like... he's really not that bad. This opinion varies depending on how the day has gone.

The reason I can write these positive things about him now is because this morning he discovered our old family photo album and looked through it for twelve hours without speaking. Today was a good day.

The little voodoo doll who fell apart at the seams,
Like something from your very worst dreams,
He just appeared one day like that maggot in your bin,
He has no eyelids, no real fingers, toes or even skin.

Little button eyes crudely stitched on with thread,
A lifeless stare that makes him look like he's dead.

Little voodoo doll, why do you cry?
Is it that pin that you've just stuck in your eye?
Because that is really hurting me,
I'd love to help you, but I can't really see!

Try to imagine an old bean bag that has been stuck on the roof of your house for ten years. It's mutated so much that it's grown arms and legs like a rotten mushroom. Give it two horrifyingly large eyes and the brain of a snail, and you have basically just created my roommate. A roommate that constantly wants attention and feels the need to use my toothbrush, or 'teeth-brush' as he calls it.

Frank loves to eat which isn't ideal when you have to carefully manage how much food you have in the house. It's not like I can pop to the shops to go and fill up the fridge. I'm not sure where the food goes when he eats it. It's not really the number one question on the list when you're looking at a living voodoo doll waddling around the house and banging into your priceless breakables.

Other than eating and asking relentless questions, Frank's favourite thing to do is to sit and look out of the window. Most of our windows are boarded up but we do have a small circular window on the third floor that I have left clear for observational purposes. He can sit and stare out of it for hours, like a puppy waiting for its owner to return. I've asked him what it is he's looking for out there, and every time he replies with the same answer. Mummy.

I stopped looking out the window for her a long time ago.

Fade

INT. Hallway. Dawn.
Edward is boarding up the windows with a hammer and nails. Frank, the living voodoo doll, is standing patiently beside him observing his every move in awe. A beam of bright light from one of the few remaining un-boarded windows is shining on Frank's face.

Frank: Can we go outside?
Edward: No.
Frank: Why not?
Edward: It's not safe out there.
Frank: But I love it outside!
Edward: Have you ever actually been outside?
Frank: No.

Sometimes Frank seems to have these false memories of things that have never actually happened. If I didn't know better, I would swear that he was created in an experiment that went horribly wrong. He has never left this house, yet he always talks about things that he couldn't possibly have any knowledge of.

I've wondered if he has some of my memories from growing up tucked away in his subconscious. I have been reading a lot of books in our library over this last year or two and believe it or not, the subject of unconscious shared memories between you and the voodoo doll created using your DNA doesn't seem to come up as much as I had hoped.

I have tried to speak to Frank about this, but my questions are always greeted with the same blank stare, a long pause and eventually a question of his own about something completely different. I think the closest I got to an answer was when he posed a question about a memory foam mattress.

Like so many other things, I think this will remain unanswered for now.

Equilibrium

Life before all of this happened isn't what I've decided to use these pages for, but in order to fully appreciate the difference between what is and what was, I think some context is needed.

My life before The War was very comfortable. I had everything I needed, my mum, my friends at school, even a cool little pet chameleon. I didn't have anything to complain about. That didn't stop me from complaining though. It's only now when I look back that I realise how good things really were.

I've been thinking a lot about how my day-to-day life looks now compared to a few short years ago and how much has changed…

A Day in A Life - Before

Morning
The days would always start in the same way. My stupid alarm clock would go off and remind me that I had to get up for school. I used to hit the snooze button until mum shouted from downstairs to tell me breakfast was ready.

Breakfast
Mum always prepared a small feast for us in the morning. We always had so much food in the house. I used to call the pantry the treat cupboard because it was packed with every type of delicious food you could imagine. After breakfast, I would feed my chameleon and then walk to school with my friend who lived around the corner.

Midday
I didn't particularly enjoy school, but I did like seeing my friends. I wasn't the most social person, but I had a small circle of friends who meant the world to me. I wasn't the smartest kid in class, but my teachers always said that I had 'potential'. Whatever that means. Most school days were pretty boring except for Fridays, because on Friday we had music class in the morning, hotdogs for lunch and film club in the afternoon.

Late Afternoon
After school, I would walk home with my friend and get started on my homework. My mum was very strict about my education. If I didn't have any homework to do, she would make me read in the library until she got home from work and then talk to her about what I had read. I used to hate it, it felt like I was being punished.

Early Evening
In the evenings, we would sit down and eat dinner together. Mum would never let me sit in front of the TV. We would sit at the dinner table and talk. Mum would speak to me about my day and occasionally she'd tell me about hers. I never really understood what she did at work. I knew she worked in a laboratory and that she did experiments, but I could never keep up with what she was telling me. She used to ask me to play guitar for her. I think it reminded her of my brother. Sometimes she would work in the evenings, but she would always make time for me.

Bedtime
Most nights I would have a cup of hot chocolate before bed. Mum didn't tuck me in anymore (at my request, I was too old for that), but she would wish me goodnight. Sometimes I would hear her come into my room when she thought I was asleep. She would kiss me on the forehead and tell me she loved me.

I miss that so much. All of it.

I think the thing I miss the most has to be when I would meet my friend Victoria at the cinema, and we would see whatever film was playing. Our local theatre only had two screens so there was never much choice, but it didn't matter what we were watching because I just adored being there. The smell of the popcorn, the feel of the folding seats, the universally hushed quiet that came over the auditorium as soon as the trailers started playing. These were always my favourite days. I used to look up at the names of the filmmakers and actors on the big screen, wishing that one day my name would be up there with them; knowing that it probably wouldn't.

Things have completely changed now.

A Day in A Life - After

Morning
The days still start in the same way. My immortal alarm clock goes off and I spend a few moments trying to figure out if everything I remember is a dream or reality. Once the cruel realisation dawns on me that this is all real, I wake up. Then I go and wake up Frank. He isn't allowed to sleep in my room, not since the time I woke up in the middle of the night and turned around to see him standing next to my bed, his eyes and mouth wide open, screaming silently. He was having some sort of night terror. Ever since then he has had his own room down the hall, that once belonged to my brother.

Breakfast
I try to ration the amount of food we eat for obvious reasons, especially Frank. For a small voodoo doll with no digestive system, he sure does like to eat. I eat twice a day, in the morning and in the evening. The water is still running so that's not a problem, and the garden provides most of what we need. The pantry is still pretty stocked with food, but because I don't know how long we've got to make it last; I try to stick to the garden crops as much as possible.

Midday
The next thing to do is to check the boards for weaknesses. Although the Dead sightings have calmed down over the last few months, you can never be too careful. I am constantly checking and reinforcing. Sometimes this involves breaking up furniture for extra materials. Luckily, we had plenty of wood stockpiled for the fireplace that I would use when I first put the defences in place.

I check all the windows and doors apart from the window in my mum's room. That door stays locked. Being literally trapped inside this house is something of a fire hazard, but it beats what's on the other side of those windows. The only window you could get out of is on the third floor, and the only external door is the back door that leads to the garden. Depending on the weather and time of the month, I might also need to harvest some food in the garden around this time of day. This has become quite tricky recently.

Late Afternoon
I keep watch from the third-floor window with a telescope. Once the news feed went down and the windows were boarded up, this was the only way I had to see what was going on out there. From that window I can see my entire street, the field behind the houses in front of us and a part of the city centre. I don't have a lot of weapons here, no guns or anything like that. I've got a few blunt instruments and knives I could use if it came to it. I did have a baseball bat but that was lost during the only time I dared to venture out of the house.

Early evening
We have our evening meal and inevitably I will be forced to converse with Frank. This could include answering anything between 20 to 50 questions about the most ludicrous topics. A recent example being "who would win if a marshmallow and a fox got into a fight?" I don't know how I'm supposed to answer that type of question. I tend to just phase out and give one-word answers. I also fill my evenings with reading books in the library. Sometimes I play guitar if the streets look clear of the Dead. Most recently I've started writing this diary. It's helping me remember some things and come to terms with others.

Bedtime

Something I need to do every night before bed without fail, is take a cup of coffee down to the basement for Spike. I will explain who Spike is soon but for now, let's just say that this is one of the most important things I do and if I don't do it, it could really jeopardise my safety.

Once that's done, it's time to put Frank to bed. This is one of the hardest things I have to do. It's a difficult task for many reasons, one of which is that Frank doesn't have eyelids so trying to get him to close his eyes is impossible. Imagine a small child high on sugar at the peak of its rush and then attempting to get it to go to sleep. This is basically my task every night.

When Frank finally crashes, I can go to sleep. Or at least I try. I don't seem to get much sleep these days. My mum is gone, my friends are probably all dead and my pet chameleon has decided to leave the comfort of his lovingly maintained cage in favour of the cold dark chimney for some reason.

I don't really have favourite days anymore.

ACT I

Act I - The Inciting Incident

This is my reckoning of the day The War started.

The day started the same as most days, I woke up to the sound of my alarm clock and hit snooze. My pet chameleon sat on my forehead and started licking my eyelids open, which meant it was time to get up. I remember feeling a small pain in my shoulder like I had been bitten by something which made me check my bed sheets for spiders or any other creature that might be crawling around in there. It was clean. Other than that, it was a pretty standard morning.

I walked to school with my friend, Victoria. I remember the weather was perfect, the streets were clear, and it was an uneventful journey. As we crossed the bridge towards school, my friend asked me if I had seen some of the strange things on the news last night. I hadn't. Mum never let me watch the news. She said that ignorance was bliss, and that all the news ever told you was what was wrong with the world. She never read newspapers and rarely watched TV unless it was with me.

Victoria said that there were some odd reports last night about a virus. It sounded like something from a film. Apparently, there were images of people with purple skin in hospitals in Spain. None of it sounded very believable. Surely, if this was a real thing everyone would be panicking. Right?

I didn't know it yet, but this was the day The War started. For us anyway. This would be my last day at school and the first day of the extraordinary life I live now.

The school day was different from normal. Our teachers all seemed really distracted. We were allowed to sit and watch films all day like it was the last day before the Christmas holidays or something. The teachers ignored any questions they were asked. We were just told to sit quietly and watch the film. None of us thought anything of it. If anything, we saw it as a positive because we weren't forced to learn how to do equations without using the calculators on our phones for once.

About halfway through the school day, we heard a few of the teachers arguing. The shouting got louder and louder until suddenly one of them burst into the classroom and screamed at us to leave. Mr. Smith told us all to run home to our parents while we still had the chance, and then bolted out of the classroom to his car. Moments later, the headteacher walked in and told us all to calm down. She pressed play on the TV remote to restart the film we had just watched and then left us alone.

A few of the kids in the class started to panic, a few of them had their noses pressed up against the glass to watch as a handful of the other teachers made their way to their cars, and a few other kids had simply retaken their seats to watch the same film they had watched twice this morning already. I didn't know what to do. Other than to suggest that this time we watched the film with the director's commentary on.

Shortly after that we heard the school's alarm bell go off. This was usually reserved for the annual fire drill. We walked out in single file like we were supposed to do in the event of a fire. When we got outside, we spotted that not all the other classes had followed. Most of them were running screaming like they had been told they were finishing early for the day. Some children were in tears and some were desperately looking around for a teacher. As hard as I tried, I couldn't see a single teacher anywhere, not even the headteacher.

After a while, the number of children crying increased. Those who were jumping for joy at the prospect of an early finish were now looking worried about the prospect of getting home. Those of us with phones quickly realised that using them wasn't an option. No one could get a connection, regardless of what network they were on. Some of the older kids started to leave, some of the younger ones had gone back inside the school despite the fire alarm still ringing louder than ever. Eventually, we started to see parents speeding their cars into the car park and running into the crowd in a desperate hope to claim their children. Once a parent had located their child, they would bundle them into the car and drive away at the same speed they entered the place. There was no attempt to help any of us or even warn us about what was happening. I started to panic about what I was going to do next.

My friend Victoria spotted me from across the playground. She made her way to me through the masses of terrified children. She told me that we had to leave now. Just as this happened, I heard the noise of two speeding cars crashing into each other behind me. It was a horribly loud and violent noise that made my blood go cold and all the noise of the playground disappear. After a brief pause, the screams of abandoned children returned louder than ever. Some of them had seen the aftermath of the accident and the bodies that had come through the windscreens. They were lying on the ground where we all lined up to be welcomed in the morning. One child let out a horrifying scream that could only mean that one of the bodies belonged to one of his parents. Before I could see anything else, Victoria had pulled me away and started marching me in the other direction.

As soon as we exited the gate at the far end of the playground, I heard a new type of scream. This wasn't the same scream as before. The screams of panic and sadness were replaced with screams of horror and fear. As I glanced back one final time, I thought I saw a purple figure in the middle of the playground. It wasn't until later that I realised what it was that I had seen.

The walk home was quite different to the walk to school that morning. The streets were no longer clear. They were now filled with cars queuing and banging into each other like bumper cars as they tried to overtake in lanes that weren't there. Every other house we passed by had families either rushing in or rushing out of them. I had never seen anything like it. I could feel the fear in the air. No one told us what was happening. We just knew that something was terribly wrong.

The sounds of cars screeching and crashing together, along with the terrified screams soundtracked the rest of our journey. The weather outside was still perfect.

We turned the corner to Victoria's street. She gave me a hug and then ran towards her house without saying a word. If I knew then what I know now, I never would have let her go.

My house was only around the corner so as soon as I saw Victoria walk through the giant hedges that surrounded her house like a fortress, I started running and didn't stop until I was outside my front door. The journey from Victoria's street to my front door seemed to last a lifetime. It felt like I was running up a mountain wearing concrete shoes. I had all these horrible thoughts racing through my mind. When I eventually arrived home, the front door was wide open.

There was no way that mum had left the door open. She would always shout at me if I left the keys in the front door or if I didn't shut the front door behind me within four seconds of arriving home. She was overly safety conscious and protective of me after my brother disappeared, which makes sense, I guess. What didn't make sense was why the front door had been left wide open. Something was wrong.

I slowly crept into the house unsure of what I was going to find. Mum's car was on the drive, but that wasn't a clear indication that she was home as she often power walked to work. Her shoes were in the hall by the front door, but she had lots of shoes. I could smell coffee but had no idea if it was fresh or simply lingering from this morning. I had no idea if she was home or not. I crept deeper into the house in an attempt to investigate further. Without thinking about it, I shouted out for her.

"Mum?"

No reply. My only option was to keep going further into the house.

This house had always made me feel safe. I always felt it had a special magic within its walls. All of that had now disappeared. For the first time in a long time, I felt afraid to be in this house. As I got halfway up the stairs, I realised that I hadn't closed the front door behind me. Just as I turned to go back down the stairs to close the door, a floorboard creaked underfoot and frightened the life out of me. I decided to leave the front door and press on up the stairs quicker than I had originally started.

When I got to the top of the stairs, I was faced with a long and narrow hallway. The same hallway that I've walked down every day of my life. I wondered why I'd never realised quite how long and narrow it was before. As I started to walk down it, the walls felt like they were closing in on me. The bedroom door at the end of the corridor felt like it was getting further away as I approached, like something you would expect to see in a carnival mirror. The hallway was pretty dark despite being the middle of the day, the inexplicable way all the walls in the house had turned black some years ago had a large part to play in this. Although, the darkness of the hallway did help to highlight one thing; there was a faint glow of light coming from underneath the bedroom door at the end of the corridor. This was mum's room and there was someone in there.

I paused to listen for movement inside the room. The silence was interrupted only by the squeaking of a mouse. As I struggled to listen for any sign of human life on the other side of the door, it dawned on me that I would need to go in there. I found myself frozen to the spot with fear. I felt those concrete shoes on my feet again, only this time, I was standing in quicksand. I noticed the faintest line of light running down the side of the door. It was open. This door was never open. Mum never liked me to see her experiments, she said that I might find some of the projects she was working on upsetting. I now understand what she meant by that.

Before I could muster the courage to open the door, the decision was made for me. I heard a loud crash from inside the bedroom. Sinking deeper into the quicksand in my mind and paralysed by fear, I couldn't move. The bedroom door swung open to reveal a figure that my terrified eyes couldn't fully focus on.

When my eyes finally focused, I saw a figure standing in front of me that I barely recognised...

It was mum, and she was panicking. I had never seen her like that before. She was usually the picture of calm, nothing ever phased her, and nothing ever made her angry these days. It turned out that glowing light I had noticed under the bedroom door was coming from a small television set that I had never noticed before. This was a worry, not that she had a TV, but because she had clearly been watching the news. Something terrible must be happening for the news to be on.

It looked like she had been packing things into a suitcase. I foolishly assumed it meant that we would be leaving together. As scared as I was about everything that had happened at school and all the horrible things that were potentially still to come, I knew that I would be OK as long as I was with my mum. I would never have guessed in a million years that she was only packing for herself and that she would be leaving me behind. She wasn't abandoning me, she made that very clear. At least I think she did. She spoke so quickly to me that it was hard to keep up and even harder to attempt to recall her words to me as I write this.

I think it was something along the lines of:

- What are you doing here?
- I thought you were safe at school.
- Something terrible is happening.
- I think I know how to stop it.
- You're going to be ok.
- Mummy loves you.
- I won't be gone long.
- There's enough food in the pantry to last you.
- This is Frank.
- Something about DNA.
- Leave a coffee cup on the windowsill at night.
- Mummy loves you.
- Stay inside no matter what.
- Don't open the front door for anyone.
- This will all be over soon.
- You need to be brave.
- I need to go now before this gets any worse.
- I'll see you very soon.
- Mummy loves you.

That was pretty much the gist of it. That I can remember. She kissed me goodbye and left shortly after that conversation.

It is not my wish to paint my mother in a poor and uncaring light, she loves me and wants to protect me. She must have had a good reason for leaving.

Nothing was ever the same after that day. I've been through so much since then, but I always find myself looking back on that day. Maybe it's because it was the last day that I woke up and everything was normal. I don't think I will ever get to experience that feeling again.

The War didn't end that day, it had only just begun.

The Antihero

Now that you've had a chance to come to terms with the reality of a talking voodoo doll, I should probably introduce another unbelievable creature to these pages.

Spike is, for want of a better word, a vampire. This may have been more difficult to believe before the Dead started to walk the Earth. However, Spike has lived in this house for a long time. His time with us predates The War by a few years. This is the story of how Spike came to live in our basement.

For as long as I can remember, my mum had cages of animals in her room. A lot of these were strange creatures that I didn't recognise but one was a bat. Not that I knew this at the time, but it was a vampire bat.

Mum told me quite casually one day that Spike was a vampire that had tried to attack her a few years ago while in his human form. She had managed to fight him off quite easily because apparently, he is only a teenager. Mum said she never had any intentions of hurting him. She said that once she had fought him off, he turned into a bat and tried to fly out of the window, but couldn't.

Mum said that she couldn't release the vampire back into the world knowing that he was going to kill people. And because she didn't have the heart to kill him, she decided to remove his teeth instead. She did this because she knew that when he transformed back into a vampire, he wouldn't be able to bite her or anyone else ever again. For weeks, the bat refused to transform. It simply hung upside down in the corner of its open cage.

Mum told me that one day she had been working on a project for hours and fallen asleep at her desk. When she woke up, she saw the teenage vampire huddled in the corner of her bedroom drinking a cup of coffee that she had left out. When she spoke to him, he looked up angrily at her and opened his mouth to expose his fangs, only they weren't there. Mum's plan had worked. When she removed the bat's teeth, she also removed the vampire's fangs.

She described him to me as a scarily thin teenager with long jet-black hair, too much eyeliner and skin so pale that he looked almost see through. As mad as he was, his toothless snarl was not as aggressive as it was designed to be. When she tried to comfort him, he leapt toward her and transformed into a bat again. Apparently, the bat was trying to bite her, but she was able to push him away with minimal effort.

I think mum started to feel bad for Spike. Although she felt she had done the right thing by removing his teeth, as this had saved an infinite number of human lives. She had also effectively ended Spike's.

Every night, before mum went to sleep, she would make a cup of coffee and leave it on her desk, and every morning it was empty. She was keeping him alive. In a way. The coffee was somehow acting as a substitute for the blood that gave him life. This went on for a long time, until one morning, she woke up to find the coffee cup was still full. It had been a hot summer night; mum went to sleep with the window open and Spike had finally flown away. I learnt about Spike for the first time the next morning. Mum was sat at the kitchen table in tears. When I asked her what was wrong, she told me all about him. I didn't understand why she was upset at the time. It's another thing that has started to make sense to me since writing these thoughts down on paper. I think it had something to do with my older brother and the way he disappeared. I can't be sure, but I think that Spike leaving the way he did probably brought back some of those feelings of loss to the surface.

That night, I saw mum take a cup of coffee up to bed with her. Every morning that week, I would see her bring down that same stone-cold cup of coffee with her into the kitchen. I would be eating my cereal and she would be sat there looking at that cup with tears in her eyes. It must have been the best part of a month that this routine went on until one morning, something different happened. Mum came down the stairs with a smile on her face. She was clutching an empty coffee cup and a piece of paper. Spike had come back, and he had written her a note. I saw what it said.

thAnK yOu foR sAviNg mE

Mum left out a cup of coffee on the windowsill every night come rain or shine. Some nights he would visit and drink the coffee and some nights he wouldn't, but mum didn't come down to breakfast in tears anymore. She knew that Spike was out there and that he was ok. That was enough for her. This went on until the day she left.

Even though mum had asked me to keep putting the coffee cups on the windowsill before she left, I didn't. I had bigger things to think about, bigger things to worry about. The day after mum left, I went to close her bedroom door and I noticed the coffee cup by the open window. For some reason this made me feel angry. Through all the panic and stress of her packing, she still found time to make a cup of coffee and leave it there for him. I closed the door and didn't think about it again.

It was a few weeks until I went in there again. I had been boarding up windows throughout the house and her bedroom window was the last one on the second floor to be boarded. It took me a while to finish securing the window. When I was done, I noticed that the coffee cup was on the floor. I bent down to pick it up and as I stood up, I saw something in the corner of the room. There was a pale white bat hanging upside down. It was Spike, I thought. It had to be.

I screamed at him. I was still really angry at this point, and I didn't have anyone to aim my anger at. Taking my frustrations out on Frank had just made me feel guilty. I kept shouting at this bat hanging from the ceiling and all it did was stare back at me. It hadn't moved the whole time. At the peak of my anger, I threw the coffee cup at it. The cup smashed on the wall and the bat finally moved. It started unsteadily fluttering around the room until it made its way out of the open door. I heard it screeching as it made its way down the hall.

I left the room and locked the door behind me. I haven't been back in there since.

It took me a little while to realise that the bat must still be in the house somewhere. All the doors and windows were either locked or boarded, so there was no way it could have got out. I searched every room in the house. I asked Frank if he had seen a bat, he walked to the front door and pointed to where the baseball bat normally lived. I tried to explain that the word 'bat' has more than one meaning, which blew his mind. He stood there pointing at the empty space where the baseball bat should have been with his face frozen in utter confusion for the rest of the night.

Finally, I noticed that the door to the basement was ajar. I really didn't want to go down there. I never liked going down there. It was dark and cold and scary. The walls were burned black from a fire we'd had years ago, and they still smelled of smoke. I took a deep breath and the anger returned, pushing me forward. I got about halfway down the basement staircase when I saw the figure of a human in the shadows. He was no longer in the form of a bat. I will never forget my first interaction with Spike in his true form...

INT. The Basement. Evening.
Spike is sitting in the shadows breathing heavily. Edward is standing on the stairs, silhouetted by the light shining through the doorway behind him.

Spike: Don't come any closer!
Edward: This is my house. You need to leave.
Spike: I'm not going back out there. Where's the lady?
Edward: She's gone.

Spike takes a moment to process this information.

Spike: How did she die?
Edward: She's not dead, she's just gone.
Spike: She took care of me, she kept me alive.
Edward: Well, she's not here anymore so she can't take care of you. You have to leave.

Spike stands up and slowly walks out of the shadows, towards the bottom of the staircase. His face becomes visible to Edward for the first time. Edward looks afraid.

Spike: I told you, I'm not going back out there. I will stay here until the lady returns and unless you want me to kill you, you will keep me alive too.

Edward pauses for a moment. He takes a deep breath and thinks carefully before delivering his next words.

Edward: Is that why she took care of you, because you threatened to kill her?
Spike: No. She took care of me because she took my teeth. She knew that by taking my teeth, I wouldn't be able to feed anymore and that if I couldn't feed, I would die. She took care of me because she's a good person and because it was the right thing to do. You're her son?
Edward: Yes.
Spike: That makes you a good person too?
Edward: Yes.
Spike: Then you will take care of me until she returns. And to show you my gratitude, I won't kill you in your sleep.

Edward turns to walk back up the stairs. Spike takes another step forward.

Spike: One cup of coffee… Every night… Until the lady returns, and I will spare you. You have my word.

To this day I have kept my end of the bargain and obviously so has he. I don't think he's the bad person he is pretending so hard to be. I don't think my mum would have looked after him if he was truly evil. I think he's scared. I think he's been out in the world since The War started, all on his own, unable to feed, and I think he's terrified. I think he came back here hoping to be looked after and he's too frightened to go anywhere else now.

I can't know that for certain, but I can't take the risk. Just because he can't bite, doesn't mean he can't hurt me. Or Frank. For now, it's easier to let him think he's won. I'll make the cup of coffee and leave it at the top of the basement staircase. I'll pretend to be afraid of him. I mean, more than I really am.

Spike hasn't transformed since I left him that night. Not that I know of anyway. The times that I have caught a glimpse of him since, he's been a bat. He just hangs there, staring at me. He doesn't speak to me unless he has to. I don't think he likes me and that's fine. I don't like him much either. I feel sorry for him. I understand that he's afraid and that he misses my mum. I even empathise with the fact that he is alone, but that doesn't mean that we're friends.

You can't hurt me now,
Not that you really want to,
I'll look after you.

Conflict

There are obviously a lot of strange and unusual things going on outside my front door as well as the odd few that are taking place on the inside of it. The world is in a terrible place right now, but today I can't help thinking about one of my own worst afflictions. It's something that has caused me a lot of problems over the years, and I tend not to discuss it with anyone. Frank has seen me struggle with this disorder many times and I always try to leave the room before his barrage of questions begin. You see, I was born with a severe case of cack-handedness.

Cack-Handed

/kak'handɪd/

Definition:

A person who is incapable of opening bin bags without spiralling into a mad rage.

It's a serious condition that doesn't get enough recognition. It might not sound like the worst thing in the world, but it can make things like finding the end piece of the sellotape or cling film an almost impossible task. You might think this isn't something that would be a concern here at the end of the world but think again. Imagine yourself sat on the toilet desperately grabbing for a fresh roll of toilet paper and being unable to peel off that all important first sheet because your useless fingers are unable to get any purchase on that tiny strip of perforated paper. Torture. Sadly, there is very little that modern medicine can do to remedy this serious condition. Most doctors had disregarded this problem of mine and have even suggested it isn't a real medical disorder.

As well as the cack-handedness, I apparently suffer with hay fever, and a rather severe case of earwax build-up. Neither of which seem to be causing me any problems in the middle of the apocalypse, although I am running low on cotton buds...

Close-up

I often wonder if Frank has any actual use or if he is purely for decoration? As far as I can tell, he doesn't need oxygen, so I don't think he has any lungs. I don't hear any heartbeat in his chest, so he doesn't have a heart; other than the little one sewn onto his chest for aesthetics. He doesn't urinate, which would indicate the lack of a bladder. So, if he doesn't have any organs, can't defecate and is able to magically make all the food he eats disappear… Why is it that every time he puts his finger up his nose, he is able to produce an ungodly amount of nasal mucus? He doesn't even look like he has a nose.

Today he showed me something he found in his invisible nostril that looked like it was pulsating. I'm very confused about where it is coming from. I know I produce a fair amount of snot myself, but honestly, some of the things Frank pulls out of his nose look like they have faces on them.

Sometimes he's green,
But sometimes he's red.
He remains unseen,
But something to dread.
He lives deep inside your nose.
How he got there?
Nobody knows.
You can pick him out with your finger,
But there's a part of him that will always linger.

Just when you think your nose is clean,
You wake up to the same old routine,
Your nose has been stocked like a vending machine,
With some obscene cuisine of red and green.

I'm always worried that Frank is going to sneeze one day, and just completely explode at the seams.

ACT II

Act II - What Happens Next

This is my reckoning of the days that followed The War starting.

I didn't get much sleep the night my mum left. I stayed up half the night watching the news. It was one crazy story after another. The later it got, the more bizarre the news stories became. Slowly, the channels started turning off. One by one, the news stories stopped. The last thing I remember before I fell asleep was a news anchor saying "Los Morados" and an image of a man. His skin was dark purple, and he looked dead, like the figure I saw in the school playground.

When I woke up, the TV channels had stopped broadcasting. The electricity was still on, but everything had just stopped. I checked online and saw that the news headlines hadn't been updated for a while, but there was one clear message across all of them. The Dead were killing the living. There were a lot more images now. Lots of shaky handheld camera phone footage and photos taken from a distance. The quality of the images didn't matter, they all showed the same thing. The end of the world.

I checked social media to see if any of my friends had reported anything. Similar to the news, the posts had stopped at some point during the night. There hadn't been anything new for hours. The last few posts I could see said things like:

Disco - "This is mental, are you seeing this?"

LL - "It's real. I've just seen dead things walking out there."

Jimi Blaze - "We're leaving, it's not safe here."

MC Mouse - "I can't believe you're all listening to this rubbish."

Jay - "Goodbye everyone. I love you all."

Jamez - "Just been bitten by a zombie. FML."

I refreshed my news feed, but there was nothing new. Everything had just stopped. I was alone.

I tried to send a message to my friend who hadn't posted anything, just to see if she was ok. As soon as I hit send, the screen started buffering and then froze. I couldn't get anything to work after that. No more news feed, no more social media, no phones, nothing. From that moment on, my only news source came from what I could see out of my windows.

Not right away, but after a while I started seeing things outside my front door. Things that I had seen glimpses of on the news, things that I had seen depicted in films and television, but never imagined I would see in real life. Things I will never forget.

Apart from cars driving and people racing past, the first thing that I saw that opened my eyes to the horrors unfolding was the dead man. I had placed a chair by the window in the living room. It's a big window that runs floor to ceiling. From that window, I could see everything outside.

At first it just looked like a man. He was walking slowly and with what looked like a limp. It wasn't until he was right outside my window that I noticed the purple face and the blood around his mouth. The blood all over his clothes, and the wounds beneath the rips in them became clear to see. The trail of blood he left behind with every other footstep. The eyeball that looked like it was about to fall out of its socket. The clumps of missing hair that had been pulled from his head. I could even see the blood-stained medical ID tag around his wrist.

Even worse than what I could see was what I could hear. The noise that thing was making was nothing like anything I had ever heard before. It was like a mix between the desperate dying breath of a man and the vicious snarl of a cornered animal. That is simply the noise they make when they are docile. I would later learn what noise they make when they lay their eyes on the living. That scream will pierce right through you and make you wish that you would never hear anything again.

It's safe to say that I had never been so scared in my life. That was until the dead man stopped walking and turned its head in my direction. It was a brief moment, but the whole world seemed to freeze. Everything started moving in slow motion. My eyes were glued to its eyes, and I couldn't look away. It had seen me. Suddenly, it felt like the brick walls and glass window in between us had disappeared. It was as if everything that was keeping me safe had melted away and I was standing right in front of this thing. I felt the blood in my veins turn stone cold. I had frozen just like the rest of the world. The dead man took a step forward. I felt a heartbeat for the first time in a while. I didn't feel another until I saw the dead man turn and continue along the path. Time seemed to speed up again like someone had hit fast forward on the remote. The walls and windows appeared in my vision again. It hadn't made any sense to me. Why hadn't the dead man walked towards me? I collapsed to the ground in a pile. Nothing felt real. Not until I woke up.

When I finally came around, I didn't want to look out of that window again because I was afraid of what I'd see. It could have only been a few hours, but it looked like a few years had passed outside. It was as if someone had put a grey filter in front of the camera lens. The audio track was filled with sirens, gunshots, and faraway screams. As time passes, I remember less and less of the next thing that happened outside that window, but the key players will have a place in my memory forever. A man was lying in the middle of the street next to a burnt-out car. He was hanging out of the passenger door with his back on the road and one leg still inside the vehicle. This man was alive. There was another man kneeling beside him, eating him as he screamed in pain. The dead man was eating out of his open stomach like it was a bowl of pasta.

A completely involuntary noise came out of my mouth when I saw this scene. There was no way that monster in the road could have heard it, but at that very moment, it stopped feasting on the man in the car and looked up. It locked eyes with me just as the first one had. It had seen me, and it was starting to stand up.

I blinked.

As my eyes opened, I saw the dead man's head fly from its shoulders. All of a sudden, my living room window turned into an IMAX cinema screen. I could see everything in crystal clear 3D, technicolour. I saw the dead man's head fall to the ground and the pool of blood around it. I saw the machete that had sliced the dead man's head clean off with ease. I saw the tattooed woman holding the blade. I saw the group of people she was with. There must have been twenty of them in total. They looked like something out of a video game, like they had been prepared for this moment. None of them saw me. I saw the group disappear down the street. I saw that the man in the car wasn't alive anymore.

I sat down again and tried to process what I had just seen. It was a living nightmare. At that point, I couldn't imagine anything worse. I realised after seeing that group, how totally unprepared I was. I remember thinking, what if mum doesn't come home? What if I have to go out there? What am I going to do?

The next time I stood up and looked out of the window, not much had changed. The car was still there, the decapitated head was still on the ground, and it looked like it was moving. The grey filter was even darker. One crucial thing was missing though. The man in the car was gone. He was dead, wasn't he? His stomach had been torn open. I saw his organs in that thing's mouth. There was no way he could still be alive. Had someone taken him away? My mind couldn't stop asking these questions that I had no chance of answering then.

As the questions continued to spin around in my head, I heard a scream. Enter stage right, the woman who would haunt my dreams for a long time. Out of all my memories of that day standing by the window, this is still the most vivid. My dreams have become much worse since back then; but for a while, she was the star of the show. I remember the colour of her hair, the bright clothes she was wearing, the bite mark on her shoulder and how it was all covered in an ocean of blood. I can still hear the sound of her voice, the slap of her body hitting the ground when she tripped, and the agonising noise she made as she pulled herself to her feet. Most of all, I remember the look on her face when she saw me at the window. She took a deep breath and screamed with everything she had left...

"Help!"

The audio turned off. The sound of sirens and screams all disappeared. What happened next, happened in silence.

The woman screamed again, and it was at that moment I noticed what it was she was running from. The Dead.

This time there were two of them. They weren't moving very quickly, but they both had a crazed look in their eyes like they were starving hungry and had just seen food for the first time in weeks. When I looked back at the woman, she hadn't moved. She was looking at me with tears running down her face creating streaks through the blood. I don't know if the tears were because she knew what was about to happen to her, because she had accepted defeat or because, despite her desperate call for help, she wasn't going to receive any. All she could see was a scared little boy standing in the window of a big house, a boy frozen stiff with tears in his eyes, silently staring at her in disbelief. That was the last thing she saw.

She didn't take her eyes off me. Not when the Dead bundled her to the ground, not when they took their first bites and not even when one of them tore her arm off. She didn't stop looking at me until one of the Dead bit right through her skull. That's when her eyes finally closed.

I don't know what possessed me to stand and watch the whole gruesome scene play out. I felt like I couldn't move away, like I needed to see this, like there was going to be some sort of post-credits scene, but there was no group of video game heroes with machetes this time. The dead men ate that woman. All of her. They didn't stand up until there was nothing but bones left on the pavement. The same pavement that I learned to ride my bike on when I was little. The same exact place where I had fallen off my bike and scraped my knee. The same concrete slab where a tiny pool of my blood had spilled was now covered with the entirety of that woman's. To this day, I have not forgiven myself for not helping her.

When the Dead had finished with their meal, they stood up and started walking with the same crazed look in their eyes. Their hunger unaltered. They were heading this way. Someone turned the audio back on. It all came flooding back and it was excruciatingly loud.

I dropped to the floor to hide from the dead men looking for their next victim. I needed to stay quiet so that they would move on. It was at that point that Frank waddled into the living room. My mum had tried to explain to me what Frank was in a hurry the night before, but I hadn't spoken to him yet. I didn't see why I should. He just stood there staring at me with those horrifying eyes. When he opened his mouth, I didn't even know the thing could speak. That wasn't one of mum's bullet points.

Most of what Frank said at that moment in the living room escapes me now. Mainly because of how shocked I was that he could actually speak, but also because I was trying to keep quiet. I remember he said he had something important to say. He mentioned my mum and brother's names. Then he said something about how my mum had created him in a lab. I remember he used the word magic a lot. The reason I'm having trouble remembering all the details is because while Frank was talking, I was desperately trying to shut him up. The universal signal of putting one's finger to one's lips and whispering "shhhh" seemed to be lost on Frank. Shouting "shut up" would have been a bit of a dangerous thing to do given the perilous situation. So instead, regrettably, I did this…

INT. The Living Room. Early evening.
Edward grabs Frank, the voodoo doll by the throat and pins him to the floor. Edward speaks quietly but with desperate rage in his voice.

Edward: I'm only going to tell you this once. You need to be quiet. There are things out there that will come and kill us if they hear you. Don't say anything. Just shut up.
Frank: But…

Edward: I told you to shut it. I'm not interested in what you have to say. I don't care what you are or why you're here. Don't you ever speak to me.

Frank looks sad.

Frank: I'm sorry.

Frank exits.

I'm not proud of that moment. In fact, looking back on that fills me with shame. It was a horrible thing to do. I wasn't thinking clearly, but that is no excuse. I have tried to speak to Frank about that day since. Firstly, to apologise, and secondly, to ask him what he was trying to tell me. Frank doesn't have any memory of that interaction, so he says. Maybe he has just blocked it out. Maybe the thought of it hurts him so he pretends not to remember. I don't know.

The dead men eventually walked away. I stood there alone until it got dark. I really started to panic about what I was going to do. Mum had mentioned there was enough food in the house, but that's not what was worrying me. I hadn't eaten all day and I didn't even notice the hunger. I had been stood by that window all day like an audience member at a beheading, watching the end of the world slowly unfold in front of me. What was worrying me was if I would remain alone or not. Would mum be coming home? She mentioned something about stopping this before it gets worse. How could it get any worse than this?

The last thing I remember about that day standing at the window was the father and son. They lived in one of the houses opposite me. I think the father was a mechanic or something, and the son wasn't much older than me. I saw them rush out of their front door with weapons in their hands. I guess they were more like tools, but they did the job and the job was killing a group of the Dead that were closing in on a young lady. They bashed the flesh-eater's heads in and helped the lady up. Before the three of them moved on, the son spotted me in the window and shouted…

"Help!"

This was a different type of cry for help. It wasn't like the desperate final cry of the woman earlier. The son wasn't in any immediate danger and didn't actually need me to help him. This was more of a demand to help the world in general. An order to do something about the awful situation we found ourselves in. At least that's what I think now that I'm looking back on it. He wanted me to do what he and his father were doing and help people. The son looked at me with disappointment in his eyes as if to say, "why aren't you helping?" He stood there until the father shouted his name. They ran away with the young lady. I never saw them again.

I woke up the next morning on the floor by the window. I don't remember it being a conscious decision to stay there for the night. I think I must have stood there looking out of the window until my body gave up and fell asleep. It wasn't the morning sun that woke me, it was the knocking at my front door. As yesterday's events came flooding back to me and I was hit in the face with the fact that they weren't part of some twisted dream, but in fact real. I got to my feet and walked to the door. Before I could reach it, the knocking turned into banging. Without giving it enough thought, I called out "who's there?" The voice that answered wasn't recognisable at first.

"Edward! It's me, Daniel. From next door. Let me in. Quick!"

Again, without thinking, I took a step forward and my hand made a move for the door handle. Finally, my brain woke up and got to work. It started its shift by asking me some questions. Who is Daniel? He's our next-door neighbour. Have you ever even spoken to him? No, I don't think so. What does he want? Maybe he wants to help. Don't you think you should find out before you open the door to him?

I called out again, "what do you want?" He replied, "I'm here to help you. Hurry up and open the door...Quick, there's a few of those things out here." I stayed silent until he spoke again. "Look, I know you're on your own in there and I know you must be scared, but I can help you if you just let me in."

For some reason, an image of the big bad wolf came to my mind. My silence brought on another round of banging on the front door and my mind pressed me for a few more answers...

How does he know that you're alone? Perhaps because mum's car isn't on the drive? Why is he making so much noise if he's so concerned with the Dead out there? I don't know, maybe he's scared too. If he's so scared, why is he coming to help you? I don't know. What did your mum tell you about opening the door? She said, don't open the front door for anyone.

The wolf at the door's tone of voice changed. Suddenly, he wasn't polite anymore. He sounded quite aggressive. "Open this door right now boy! I mean it. Open the door!" Again, I greeted his request with silence. The sound of banging was upgraded once again. He started kicking at the door. I opened the cupboard under the stairs and grabbed the first sensible item I could find, which was a black steel baseball bat. The front door didn't look like it was going to budge at all, but I gripped the bat as tight as I could. The wolf's tone changed one last time, now sounding panicked. I don't remember his exact words, but it sounded like he had seen something. He swore. The next thing I heard was his footsteps running away. I quickly moved back to my window to see what was happening. I saw the Dead the wolf must have seen and that they were moving towards him. Another neighbour gone, never to return home.

The Dead kept coming. More and more of them staggered past the window. I recognised some of them. Neighbours. People who worked in the local shops. I even saw our postman go past in his uniform. It wasn't until I saw one of the kids from my class walk past that I started to think about Victoria. The three of us were in the same class at school. The kid who walked past my window wasn't exactly a friend of mine, but he was someone I saw almost every day. He was a smart kid, popular, funny, and good at sports. Dead.

I couldn't stop thinking about Victoria. The last time I saw her, she was running into her house. She must be safe. I'm sure she's with her mum and dad and that she's ok. What if she isn't? What if when she got home there was no one there? What if she went back out to look for her parents? What if she's still out there?

I had to find out.

I thought that the only way I could get answers was by going out there myself and looking for her. It wasn't that far away. Victoria's house was only around the corner. I could run over there and back in only a few minutes. I've done it hundreds of times. If she's on her own, I could bring her back here and look after her until mum gets back. If she's with her parents, maybe they could look after me for a while.

I thought about it for what felt like hours. Eventually my questions turned dark. What if she's not there? What if she's been killed? What would I do if I saw her body out there?

I had to save her.

I made up my mind. I would run to her house as quickly as possible, see if she was there and if she was safe. Then I would either stay there with her or run back. With or without her. I thought about what I would need to take for the journey. What if we became trapped somewhere? Should I take food? What if I came face to face with one of the Dead? Should I take a weapon?

I realised that I hadn't let go of the baseball bat. My hands were still firmly gripping the bat from when the wolf was at the front door. Decision made; I would take the bat. I loaded my school backpack with crisps and chocolate bars from the treat cupboard. As I was filling my bag I stopped and looked at the kitchen knives. As I reached out to grab one, I suddenly thought, would I be able to do it? Those Dead that I had seen from my window were the scariest things I had ever seen in my life. If one was stood in front of me, what would I be able to do? There is a strong possibility that I am going to be faced with that situation. I guess that's why mum told me to stay inside no matter what.

But I couldn't leave Victoria out there. She's my friend.

I walked to the front door and Frank was standing there staring at me with that medically gormless look of his. He said, "She told me not to let you go." I chose to ignore him. I moved him aside with ease, took a deep breath and opened the front door.

I took one step outside onto our porch and before I could even close the front door behind me, I saw one. A dead girl. Similar age as me, similar height. I nearly choked as the camera pulled focus and I could see her face. It wasn't Victoria, but it could have been. She was just clumsily staggering down the road with no aim in sight. She hadn't seen me. Not yet. Even if I had wanted to take a second step, my body wouldn't let me. Those concrete shoes were back on my feet and heavier now than ever before. My body started to shake, and I could feel tears starting to pour down my face. I had seen the Dead from the safety of my window, but it had been like seeing them on the big screen. This was different. This one was real, in 4K, right in front of me. I crumbled completely. The dead girl turned her gaze in my direction, and I felt a storm fill my lungs like I had just jumped out of a plane. I instantly snapped out of it and hurried behind my front door. I slammed it shut and bolted it with the intention of never opening it again.

I was a coward. I am a coward. I don't blame you if you hate me. I hate myself for that day. I could have done something. I might have been able to save someone's life that day. Instead, I lay down on the floor in the hallway and cried like a scared child. I wonder how many people died that day, how many people I might have been able to help. I remember Frank lying down next to me and not saying a word.

At some point, towards the end of my break down, I heard an explosion far off in the distance. I couldn't see anything from my window, so I went upstairs. Nothing from the bedroom window either. I climbed the stairs again to reach the third floor. Mum keeps a telescope up there, although I don't think I've ever seen her use the thing. I looked through it and couldn't believe what I saw.

From up there, I could see everything. I could see all along my street, I could even see as far as the centre of town. This is where most of the action was taking place. This is where the explosion must have come from. A lot of the shops were on fire, shops that I would go to every weekend to spend my pocket money. The place was swarming with people. The living and the Dead. It was different to what I had seen from my living room window. I saw people running into shops, grabbing electronics and other valuable items. I saw them running out of the shops, only to be greeted by a horde of the Dead.

Unlike what I had seen take place outside my house, the Dead would take down a living person, start eating them and then get distracted by another one. They would rarely finish a meal before moving onto the next one. It was through the telescope that I saw a full transition take place. A man that had come running out of a shop holding a big screen TV was taken down by one of the dead ones, a few bites were taken out of his neck and torso before the dead person moved onto its next course. The TV man lay still for a few minutes before his body started to twitch. He looked dead. He was dead. I saw that TV man stand up and start walking. He had become one of the army of the Dead in a matter of minutes.

It's as I feared. It must be what happened to that man in the car outside my house. They turn when they've been bitten.

I moved the telescope in the direction of the school playground. It was a sea of purple. It looked like they had all been trapped inside. All the gates were shut. The Dead were just aimlessly shuffling around, not trying to escape, not trying to do anything. As you might expect, the playground was full of children. I spent a few minutes looking to see how many I could recognise. After I put a few names to dead faces I had to step away from the telescope to be sick into a pair of nearby shoes. Looking at all those faces of the school children once again made me worry about Victoria. I knew I wouldn't see her face in amongst the never-ending assembly of poor dead students. I knew she wasn't there because we left together. She must be at home. She must be.

Victoria's house was around the corner from mine, meaning that whichever way I directed the telescope, I couldn't see it. I don't know what I was expecting to see anyway. Maybe Victoria sitting at her bedroom window with her parents stood behind her, waving at me as if to say that everything was alright and that this would have blown over by tomorrow, and we could all get together to bake cookies. That isn't what I could see in any direction I pointed the telescope. Everything was quite the opposite.

This was all horrifyingly real now. There was no avoiding it. This wasn't going to be resolved anytime soon. Another loud explosion in the city centre forced me from my seat. I couldn't watch anymore. I removed my backpack and took out some of the crisps that I'd packed for my failed journey. As I ate, I thought of Victoria and kept telling myself the same thing. She would be ok. She would be safe. I hope she's ok. I hope she's safe.

She must be.

The Script

The few news stories I heard before everything switched off referred to them as 'Los Morados'. Loosely translated, it meant 'The Purple Ones'. I think they were desperate to avoid the word 'Zombie' due to its connections with works of fiction. I just call them 'the Dead'.

So, what are they? They are exactly what they say on their tin. Dead. I don't mean that dead people started to dig themselves out of their graves they've been slowly rotting away in. I mean, they were recently alive, they got bitten by a dead person, they died and then they came back. Reanimated. When I say they came back, I do not mean that they came back to life. That's not what happens. I mean, they come back as the Dead. Let me try and break it down into three easy steps...

Step 1: Patient Zero (who remains unknown at this time) is the first person to reanimate. How this happens is still a mystery and it's a very big missing piece of our little puzzle here.

Step 2: Patient Zero is now a walking dead person who's only goal in afterlife is to feed on living human beings. I don't think they aim to kill. I have seen them eating people who are still alive.

Step 3: Patient Zero manages to bite a living human. The virus/disease/bug (whatever you want to call it) is passed on to that living human. Once said living human ceases to be living, they then come back as a dead person themselves.

This process is then repeated over and over until there are no living human beings left. This is my current position on the timeline. I don't know how it started. None of the news stories managed to give a clear answer to that burning question. Although I have managed to learn a lot about them from looking through my telescope and studying them, I still haven't been able to figure out how it started. I don't think I ever will. What I have learned is that these things are almost unstoppable.

I have seen people trying to defend themselves by stabbing the Dead through the heart and the Dead just keep on going. I have seen them with limbs cut off, mortal wounds, even cut in half. A dead person with their entire lower half missing, still crawling along the floor in search of food. The only way to stop them is to kill the brain. If you kill the brain, they die. Permanently. I know this because I've had to do it myself.

The dead people are very easy to recognise, but just in case, I have put together this handy little guide to help you spot them when you're out and about…

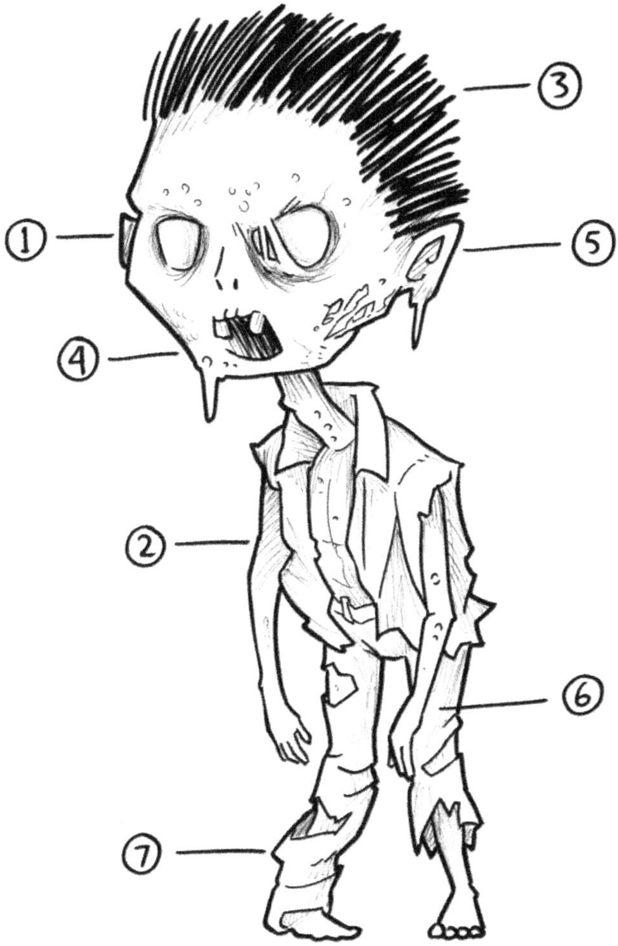

fig 1. Eyes
The Dead can see you but not very well. The problem is that once they have seen you, they don't unsee you. They will follow you until they end you, or until you end them. They are also attracted to bright lights and can be distracted. I saw a group scavenging in the city save themselves by setting fire to a shop opposite to them and then making their escape. The Dead just walked right into the fire.

fig 2. Body
Their bodies just don't seem to take damage. They are practically invincible. As I mentioned, I've seen one get stabbed through the heart and just keep on moving forward like nothing happened, much to the surprise of their victim. You can cut their throats and even remove their internal organs. Nothing stops them other than killing the brain.

fig 3. Brain
Their brains are not human anymore. There is nothing left of the people they once were. I have seen a mother eat her own child after turning. Once they are dead, the person they once were is gone forever. The brain can function even when the head has been removed from the body. The brain must be destroyed otherwise the severed head can still bite and infect you.

fig 4. Teeth
This is how they get you. If you watch them move, they lead with their mouths. It's like they have a magnet in their mouths that is constantly pulling them towards the living, like a compass pointing them in the right direction. Once they have bitten you, it's over. You will turn into one of them.
Do not let them bite you.

fig 5. Ears
This is how they find you. They don't rely on their eyesight or their sense of smell. They use their ears to find you. Loud noises will obviously get their attention. At the start, the city centre was nothing but noise. Sirens, gunshots, screams, explosions. This attracted the Dead like moths to a light. They will also hear the slightest sounds too. If you are hiding, you need to make sure that you are silent.

fig 6. Skin
You can tell that someone has joined The Dead Club simply by looking at their skin as it will have turned purple. This is where 'The Purple Ones' came from. I have no idea what causes this. You can also get a good idea of how long they have been dead for as their skin will start to rot away.

fig 7. Legs
These things don't move very quickly. I have seen some move faster than others. I think it depends on the person they were before they died. If they were a healthy young adult, it makes sense that they would have strong muscles and therefore, move quite quickly. If they were overweight and on the brink of a heart attack, presumably they would be much slower. They tend to speed up considerably when they have seen a human, but they are still quite slow. I think their movements also depend on how long they have been dead for. The recently deceased ones move a lot easier than the ones that are starting to rot.

I think the most terrifying thing about the Dead is how quickly and how easily it is to become one of them. I have kept myself locked away, I have been very careful, and I am a coward. I know that all it takes is one bite. They don't even need to kill you. I saw someone get bitten on the roof of a shop in the city while trying to close the emergency fire exit door up there. I saw him collapse and I saw him pass out. Less than an hour later I saw him stand up and walk off the roof of that three-storey building and splatter in a pool of blood on the concrete floor below. Sometimes it takes a while for them to turn, sometimes it happens almost instantly. It may depend on how deep the wound is. It doesn't matter how careful you are, how well protected you are or even how safe you think you have made yourself. All it takes is one bite and you will be welcomed into The Dead Club with open arms.

Lighting

In all honesty, the reason I think I have survived this long is because of this house. There is something about it that protects me, it's hard to explain. I've been thinking about a few rules I live by that might help someone who finds these pages.

Survival Rule #1 - Keep the Lights Low

The Dead follow light. This isn't a problem during the day, but at night, you need to make sure your fortress is kept dark.

We have a backup generator in the basement which to this day still powers the house along with the help of my pet chameleon, which is another thing I will explain later. Mum used the generator for her experiments. At least, that's what she said. A part of me thinks she knew something like this would happen one day and was planning for it. She really did build a fortress for us.

Sometimes it feels like there is some kind of magical force field surrounding this house. I have seen the Dead walking towards it when the lights are on at night, but before they get to the front door, something stops them, and they just walk away.

I guess it could be something to do with the gargoyle that sits on top of the house. He suffers with a syndrome that makes him shout appalling things at anything that passes by the house. For the longest time I was worried that he would attract unwanted attention but to this day, nothing dead has ever attempted to get into this house. Maybe it's a coincidence, maybe it's just dumb luck that the Dead haven't tried to get inside this house. Maybe it's only a matter of time.

I wonder how long I would have survived without this house; how I would have coped if I was out in the streets? I hope I never find myself in that situation. For now, I am doing what my mum told me to do. Stay home and stay safe.

I can't help but wonder though, if this house is so safe, why did she have to leave?

Cameo

When I was little, my big brother used to tell me stories about the Tooth Troll. The other kids at school would say that they were visited by a fairy, and that they were given money in exchange for their baby teeth. This is not how the Tooth Troll operated.

The Tooth Troll only appears in the dead of night,
He sticks to the shadows and stays out of sight.
If you're not in bed and asleep in time,
Then upon your bed the troll will climb.

The Troll's aim is to remove the teeth right from your jaw,
So that you will be eating the rest of your meals through a straw.
He's not interested in the loose teeth that you've left out for the fairy,
He wants the attached ones and how he removes them can be quite scary.

As a punishment for you breaking your curfew,
He'll kick your mouth with his steel toe-caped shoe.
So, make sure you're in bed tonight before ten,
Or the Tooth Troll will be coming back again.

I didn't really think it was real. I just thought my brother was making it up to frighten me, but sometimes I would wake up in the morning and my teeth would feel loose. I didn't actually think that there was a small troll that was kicking my teeth out in my sleep. Not until I lost my last baby tooth. I went my whole life without seeing the Tooth Troll but on my twelfth birthday, after going to bed late, I woke up in the middle of the night and felt a pain in my mouth. I could feel a gap in between my teeth where my last baby tooth had been. I opened my eyes and saw this little ugly creature with wings holding a bloody tooth in his arms. I was very tired and probably just dreaming, but it looked like he was crying. I think he wanted to say goodbye.

Dream Sequence

I seem to find it extremely difficult to sleep at night. I would honestly rather stay awake at night than go to sleep because when I sleep, I dream, and when I dream, I have nightmares. I don't remember the last time I managed to sleep without having one.

I have a reoccurring dream where I am standing at the top of my staircase looking down at the front door and all I can see is black. There are no pictures on the walls. The walls themselves are shrouded in darkness, and there is nothing around me but the staircase. I feel freezing cold like I am stood outside with no clothes on. I also feel a pain in the soles of my feet like I have been walking for miles with no shoes on. I can smell the horrible scent of rotting flesh, as if I am surrounded by hundreds of dead bodies. The smell intensifies as the dream goes on and it gets so bad that I can even taste the smell in the back of my throat.

Everything is silent for a long time. I am just standing there, with nothing happening. After a while, I start to hear a banging at the front door. The banging starts softly and slowly, but it starts to build up and get louder. The banging gets so loud that it wakes me up. Those are the good nights. I wake up in a cold sweat thinking that there is someone or something at the front door.

The bad nights happen when the noise doesn't wake me up because those are the nights where the dream continues. The banging gets louder and faster, as if more and more people are getting involved. Just as I think the noise couldn't possibly get any louder, the front door breaks down and a horde of the Dead burst through the open doorway and towards the bottom of the stairs. I am unable to move. I can't run away, and I can't defend myself. I want to, but I can't, no matter what I do. It looks as though the doorway has expanded as an impossible amount of the Dead pour in. At first it looks like the usual sea of purple, but as the horde starts moving up the stairs, I start to recognise their faces.

This is where the dream differs. The horde is usually built up of school friends and distant relatives, but there is always one member of The Dead Club in the foreground of the shot, and that person changes each time. Sometimes it's my brother, sometimes it's my mum. It's occasionally Frank, which is very strange. I mean it's weird enough seeing Frank in his normal form, let alone as a rotting purple dead thing. The worst is always when the dead person in focus is Victoria. I hate it.

The army of the Dead keep slowly marching their way up the stairs. The staircase seems to get wider and wider, which allows even more of them to fit into the frame. There is now a terrifyingly large amount of them coming towards me with that look of desperation in their eyes, but there is still one person leading the pack, and it is that person that reaches me first.

Up until this point in the dream, everything has been filmed in a single point-of-view shot. Just as the Dead are about to reach me, the camera pulls back and shows a lovely over the shoulder shot so that I can see them grab me and pull me down into the centre of the horde. It doesn't end there though. I watch as they all rip into me at once. I have to watch as my body is pulled apart and my organs are gorged on. Just when it looks like I am about to die, the lens fills with blood, and I wake up.

I've had the dream so many times now that it makes me not want to go to sleep. No matter how many times I experience the dream, I don't get used to it. It's always just as horrible. Although part of me knows what's going to happen, when I'm there in the moment it feels real. Every time.

I am writing this right now to avoid having to go to sleep.

Subplot

<u>The Little Werewolf - A story by Edward</u>

Little Vinny was one of the happiest boys in the world. Until one day, while playing in the front garden, little Vinny was attacked by a big scary wolf. The wolf mauled little Vinny half to death. It took a bite out of his throat and ripped one of his arms from its socket. Little Vinny cried in pain, but no one came to save him.

When the wolf finished feeding on little Vinny's body it ran away, leaving the poor little boy pouring with blood. Despite this savage attack and being in excruciating pain, little Vinny didn't die. He lay on the cold ground, struggling to stay awake, hoping and praying that someone would find him. But no one came to save him.

Very slowly and painfully, little Vinny was transformed. His bones cracked as they grew under his flesh, his skin tore as it stretched over his expanding muscles. His teeth broke off and fell out of his jaw to make room for his fangs. His fingers extended into terribly sharp claws. Little Vinny had transformed into a werewolf.

As Vinny the werewolf stood up for the first time, he struggled to keep his balance. He turned and saw his family home and part of him wanted to go inside. He heard a scream from a terrified passerby who had seen his new form. Something in his mind told him he couldn't go back home. Little Vinny had transformed into a werewolf.

The little werewolf ran away from his family home as fast as he could. He was scared and confused about what had just happened and everything in his body was hurting him immensely. His vision was blurred, and he didn't know where he was going. But most of all, he was hungry.

After hours of running in no particular direction, the little werewolf found himself in a dark and damp sewer. He was cold and alone. He didn't know where he was. He was frightened. Not just because of the transformation and the pain he was in, it was also because he had never been away from his family before. But most of all, he was hungry.

The wolf part of his brain was telling him he had to find meat. He tried to fight the thoughts that were filling his head. He knew he had to eat but he didn't want to eat people. As time went on, he realised he had no choice, the animal instinct within him was too powerful a voice.

About three years before The War started, my older brother Vincent disappeared. Vincent was a few years older than me. To this day, we don't know what happened to him. I wrote the story about the werewolf not long after he left. I think I wrote it about my brother to bring me some kind of comfort. I know it is extremely unlikely that he was bitten by a wolf and transformed, but up until a few years ago it would have been considered extremely unlikely that the Dead would be walking the Earth and that getting bitten by them could transform you into one of them.

I wish I knew what happened to him. Even if he is dead, I just want to know. Everyone assumes he is because it's been so long since his disappearance, but for some reason, I have never been able to accept it. I don't think about him as much as I used to now that there are dead people wandering around outside, but I will never forget him. I know the story I wrote about his disappearance isn't very nice, but it's a lot nicer than some of the things that could have happened to him. I like the story because it contains hope. Some sort of hope that he is still out there somewhere, and that he's alive. I have never given up on that hope. There is some foolish part of me that still thinks he is out there somewhere.

As time goes on, my memories of him become hazy but there are certain things that have stayed with me. He loved music, films, video games and painting models. He was always making up stories and trying to scare me. Things like the Tooth Troll, the Gleeken and the Earwax Pixie. He was never nasty about it. It was just his way of having fun with me. I know he loved me really. He just made it a bit difficult for me to get to sleep at night.

When he disappeared, my mum was distraught. It was always just the three of us. Our dad wasn't around when we were growing up. Whenever we asked mum about what happened to our dad, she would just smile and say that he died during childbirth. I never understood that joke. I still wonder if he's out there somewhere too. I don't have any memories of him.

For a long time, my mum searched for my brother. She wouldn't do anything else. Even when the police called off their search and basically told her that finding him was a lost cause. She never gave up. She never wanted to. The search for him felt like it had been going on forever.

Mum became quite ill. She wasn't taking care of herself properly. Although I was still very young at the time, I know that I asked her to stop searching. I could see what it was doing to her, and I was worried. I remember her looking at me with tears in her eyes. She grabbed me and held me so tight. She didn't talk about Vincent very much after that day. Understandably, mum was still so sad for such a long time afterwards, but she did stop searching. She became very protective of me. Which is why it was so out of character for her to leave me alone like this. Whatever it is she had to leave for must have been extremely important.

I haven't thought about the little werewolf for such a long time. With everything that's been happening over the last few years, the story just became buried in the back of my mind along with so much more. I'm not sure why I thought about it today. Maybe it has something to do with Frank looking through all those photo albums last week. Mum didn't keep pictures of Vincent around the house because they made her too sad, but she did keep them in the photo albums. Although the photo albums kept Frank pretty quiet that day, he did ask me one question.

"When can we go back to the seaside?"

He was looking at a photo of me, mum, and Vincent at the beach. I still don't understand how Frank's memories work. When I asked him, he struggled to explain. He just said that he remembered being with mum at the seaside and that seemed to make him happy. He also says something similar about eating sugar straight from the jar so it's difficult to know how serious he's being when he tells me these things.

I know I shouldn't blame myself for Vincent's disappearance, I was only young when it happened. Even though I know there's nothing I could have done, I still feel guilty. I think I feel guilty that I got to have a normal life. At least up until recently. Whatever reason took him away, I don't think it was because he didn't want to be with us. He was always so happy. At least I thought so. He did run away once, about a year before, but I don't remember him being gone long. When he came back, he told me stories about how he had gone on a ship to somewhere far far away. We don't think he ran away this time because he didn't take anything with him when he left. His things are still in his bedroom. I see it all every day when I put Frank to bed. He sleeps in Vincent's room. I've kept everything the way it was in there. I figured that when Vincent came back, he wouldn't be happy if I had moved things around in there. He never did like me playing with his toys unless he was there to play with me. Vincent's bedroom walls are still covered with the polaroid photos he had taken. I find it comforting to see them every day.

I miss him. I wish for a lot of things, especially with the way the world is now. I have always wished that my brother is OK and that one day, I will see him again.

Foreshadowing

The Meaning of Life: Frank really shocked me today. His consistently, irritating questions are usually along the lines of what purple tastes like and why doesn't he ever have to use the toilet? Today was different, he asked me what his purpose is, why is he here and what is the meaning of life?

I found this very difficult to answer. How am I supposed to know what the meaning of life is? I remember asking my mum a similar question when I was little. She told me she could answer that question using only three words...

Love, Dream, Create.

I didn't understand that when I was young, I'm still struggling to understand it now. I attempted telling Frank those three words and he stared blankly at me for a while and then asked me why worms don't have legs. This was disappointing. I finally thought that Frank might be maturing and that we might be able to have an intelligent conversation for once. I asked him if he could pick three words to describe the meaning of life, what would they be. He thought about this for a moment and then replied...

Food, Tummy, Yum.

I don't know what caused Frank to ask me a real question today. Needless to say, it was not due to a sudden increase of intelligence.

One of the last things I remember my brother Vincent telling me, in a way, was his version of what he believed to be the meaning of life...

Life is Imagination.

I think that one makes the least sense of them all, but it's probably my favourite.

The Meaning of Death: Death is waiting for me. He's been waiting for a long time. I know this because I can see him outside my window. I don't mean metaphorically; I mean he is literally standing outside of my house. He started hanging around out there earlier this year following an incident involving a villain. I can see him out there right now. Sort of. I can see a hooded figure with no face. All I can see when I look at him is this bright white skull with two black holes where the eyes should be.

It was terrifying the first time I saw him out there, standing next to that burnt out car. He was looking down at his wristwatch and then he lifted his head and looked me right in the eyes. Sort of.

I'm used to it now. The first time that I saw him, I assumed I was about to die. I thought that he was here because my time was up. That would have made sense but that was a while ago now and he's still out there. I have checked with Frank to make sure that he can see him too, so I know that I'm not just imagining it. Although Frank does also claim that he can see a lot of things that don't actually exist, so I don't really know what to believe.

I know Death comes for all of us eventually. That being said, he's surely got other people to visit. The fact that he's been waiting for me for so long, does that mean that there is no one else? Am I the last one?

It's a scary thought and I sincerely hope it's not true, but it would explain why he's waiting for me. Is the reason that Death is waiting for me, because everyone else is already dead?

Major Dramatic Question

I wonder how many people in the world have survived this apocalypse?

It's a big question, but perhaps an even bigger question is…
Why do I keep getting so much bellybutton fluff?

That's the major dramatic question.

I found so much this morning, I could have sworn there was something living in it…

This creature's name is Fluff and he lives in your bellybutton.
He is always the same colour as your shirt,
With the mixed texture of both cotton and dirt.

You can throw him away,
But he'll always be back the next day,
Don't worry through, he's not always that hairy,
Although sometimes he can look quite scary.

These aren't exactly the post-apocalyptic problems I thought I would be facing. I can't help but think about all the people that had to fight for their lives, had to fight to protect their loved ones. I doubt they had to worry about excessive bellybutton fluff or the fact that they are running dangerously low on cotton buds to clean their ears.

Dialogue

I should probably explain the aforementioned gargoyle that lives on the roof. Sometimes I forget that these things aren't actually normal for everyone.

There is a gargoyle that sits on top of our house, and he is incredibly grumpy. He's been up there for as long as I can remember. I don't seem to remember him shouting abusive comments when I was little, although now that I think about it, I do remember my mum sometimes having to cover my ears when leaving the house.

Mum always said the gargoyle's name was Larry, but whenever I tried to speak to him, he would introduce himself as Upyours. I just always thought that was some sort of exotic name. He has a strong regional accent which can be tricky to follow. I'm going to stick with Larry for the purposes of this story.

I remember once when I was little, I was being chased home by three bullies. I don't recall why they were chasing me, but when I got to my house, Larry jumped down from the roof and frightened them away. It is the only time I have ever seen him leave the roof. I noticed that as he was shouting insults at the retreating youths, his already rough exterior was starting to turn to stone. Before I could thank him for helping me and ask him if he was ok, he muttered something inaudible and slowly and uncomfortably made his way back up onto the roof. Later, my mum explained that Larry has to stay on top of the house and that if he leaves, he will turn to stone.

Larry acts as a sort of alarm for me now. I know that the Dead are approaching the house when he starts shouting abusive slurs at the top of his voice. Some of the things he shouts are pretty bad. He manages to get quite in depth and personal with his insults. I wouldn't be surprised if the reason the Dead turn around and walk away is due to the emotional abuse they have just suffered.

There have been a few times where I have been in the back garden harvesting supplies when Larry has started screaming words I have never heard before. This can be confusing because it's unclear if he's hurling the abuse at me or something else he's seen. I won't attempt to write down some of the more creative words I have heard him say, not just because they are awful, but because I wouldn't know how to spell them.

The plus side to having this built-in alarm on top of the house is that I know when to turn down the lights or stop playing the guitar. The downside is when

Frank overhears certain words and tries to copy them like a parrot. He doesn't understand what he's saying and more often than not, he will get the words wrong.

Part of me feels sorry for Larry the gargoyle. I don't think he can control what he's saying, and I think that deep down, he is trying to protect us by warning us when danger is near. He never seems very friendly, but behind his gravely exterior, I think he is someone that really cares about us.

It is sometimes difficult to remember that though when he is calling me a "massive sponk bobble". Whatever that means.

Jump Scare

INT. The Kitchen. Dusk.
Edward is blowing up a balloon. Frank enters stage right.

Frank: Please don't burst that balloon.
Edward: Why?
Frank: I have a phobia.
Edward: Of what?
Frank: Spiders…

It's a funny thing, I'm not sure that I'm afraid of anything anymore. Except maybe buttons. Ever since I met Frank and saw his button eyes stitched onto his head, I've developed a bit of an irrational fear of them. Oh, and the cupboard under the stairs. I'm afraid of the cupboard under the stairs too, for reasons that won't help you gain any respect for me. But that's it. The dead people walking around outside scare me, but not as much as they used to. At least that's what I tell myself. I locked myself away for a long time because I was afraid. I might have been able to help people if I hadn't been so scared. I certainly could have helped at least one person. Sadly, I know this for a fact.

Sometimes, you don't know you're afraid of something until you are faced with it for the first time. I remember my mum took me on a helicopter ride when I was little. It was one of those big ones with a glass floor so that you could see everything underneath you. We were part of a tour group of about six other people. As soon as the helicopter took off, I started to feel a bit funny. Two minutes into the journey, I threw up all over the glass floor. That pretty much ruined the trip for everyone. The journey was thirty minutes and apparently, they couldn't land anywhere else, so we all had to sit in there with the smell of my vomit which was obstructing the view of everything beneath us. Needless to say, I quickly developed a fear of heights, and I never went on another helicopter ride. I remember seeing rescue helicopters shortly after everything started. I wasn't in a position to get on one, but I always wondered if I would have been able to force myself to overcome my fear and ride one again. I guess other than buttons, the only other real thing to fear now is death. I don't think I do though. I know I don't want to die, but at the same time, I'm not afraid to. I can still see Death standing out there waiting, looking at the little watch on his bony wrist. I don't know why, but something tells me I need to stay alive. I know it's what my mum would have wanted. Death is just going to have to wait.

Exterior

It's true that I haven't been outside of this house for a very long time, but that's only if you don't count the garden. Although the pantry was stocked with enough dried food to last a trip to Mars and back, it wouldn't last forever. Once again, my mum had planned for this. She had a garden filled with basically every type of food you can grow in the ground along with a creepy looking scarecrow with a pumpkin for a head to scare the life out of any creature that dared to come anywhere near the vegetables.

I have been tending to this garden since she left with the help of my pet chameleon who likes to spend time out there when he's not hanging out in the chimney. Something about him helps the plants grow, which is another thing I will have to explain later. The garden provides enough food to keep me going. The only downside is that it has become quite dangerous to go out there. This is due to the dead garden gnome that lives out there somewhere.

He's been out there for the last few months. I have no idea how a garden gnome could have gotten turned. All I can think is that he was bitten by the Dead just like a human. My mum had loads of garden gnomes in the back garden. They all seem to have disappeared now, but I can guarantee it's one of those. It's a safe bet that he came from the secret garden. There is a maze of trees and plants located at the back of our regular sized garden. The regular garden is used for the crops. I don't go into the secret garden anymore. It's a labyrinthian mess of land and it's something I have never managed to find the back of. My brother and I used to play in it when we were little, and mum always said that there was a hidden treasure in the centre of the maze that we could keep if we ever found it. The only things we ever found in that network of twisted trees and poisonous plants were strange little creatures that used to frighten me. I'm sure the missing army of garden gnomes must be hiding back there now, and the dead one probably roams the maze whenever he isn't madly charging towards me as I'm tending to the crops.

The dead garden gnome is quite a scary looking thing, but he's also quite small. On more than one occasion I have been digging up vegetables and he has come running at me screaming with his tiny arms in the air. I simply kicked him square in the face and sent him flying. It's not that much of a challenge to be honest. Still, it does worry me that one day he might catch me off guard and actually bite me.

I wonder if I would turn into the Dead if I was bitten by a garden gnome. That really would be a bad way to go. Frank doesn't go out into the garden anymore; he's terrified of the dead gnome. I don't blame him. I don't love the idea of having a dead garden gnome roaming around out there. But on the plus side, he does keep the rats away from the vegetables. He eats them alive.

Blackout

In the old days, I never understood people that said they got bored. Adults who'd say they didn't know what to do with themselves when they were off work. There used to be so much to do. Films, TV, books, games, music. The list was literally endless, and yet people managed to get bored of it. There was nothing boring about life before The War. I bet all those people that said they were bored changed their minds pretty quick when they found themselves running away from the Dead.

Survival Rule #2 - Don't Get Bored

You need to keep yourself entertained, don't allow yourself to become bored with everyday life.

Things are different now. Although we have electricity, (as long as the magical partnership between the generator and my pet chameleon lasts), we don't have much else. There is no internet, which means no social media. I'm sure there were a lot of people that would have struggled to survive without that. I don't miss it at all. I do miss the cinema. There's nothing new anymore. We have a library full of books which is my main source of entertainment. My mum also has an old record player and a small collection of vinyl that I play. That really is it though. All our other media was digital, so when the internet went down, so did everything else.

I don't allow myself to get bored. I need to keep myself busy otherwise I start to overthink my situation and fall into the darkness. I start to think about how I might be the only person left alive in this world. How I can't leave the house because my mum told me to stay safe. My mum, who I haven't seen for years. I start to think about all these weird things that live with me in this house. This magical fortress that has somehow managed to keep away the Dead for all this time. I think about the future and what will happen to me when I get older...

That's when I stop thinking.

Costume

I put a fresh T-shirt on this morning, and I was greeted with a very strong scent that can only be described as sick. I know the T-shirt is clean because I took it out of the washing machine only yesterday. I decided to investigate the washing machine to see if I could find an explanation.

This next one is going to sound like a bit of a stretch,
But I want to tell you about a little creature named Retch.
This horrible thing lives inside your washing machine,
And its job is to stop your clothes from ever smelling clean.

When the washing cycle finally starts to slow up,
This dizzy creature tends to make itself throw up,
It's invisible sick spins around the machine like a comet,
Seeping into your clothes and making them all smell like vomit.

I knew there had to be a reason for this. For weeks now my clothes have smelt like puke when I've taken them out of the machine. I just assumed that Frank had been regurgitating the teabags he finds at the bottom of the bin into my drawers again.

I don't understand where all these creatures are coming from.

Special Effects

INT. Edward's kitchen. Daytime.
Frank is laying on the floor surrounded by cookie crumbs. Edward enters stage left. He is visibly frustrated.

Edward: Frank, have you eaten all the cookies?
Frank: Yes…
Edward: The special cookies that I specifically told you not to eat?
Frank: I feel like snow.
Edward: Brilliant. And I feel nothing. Yet, every time you decide to play 'what does this taste of?' with the things you find on the floor, I get sick for a week.
Frank: Cookies yum.

Edward exits.

The less said about the 'special cookies' and how they found their way into the pantry the better. For some reason, this event got me thinking about whether or not Frank is going to live forever? What's going to happen to him when I'm not around? If he gets bitten and turned into a card-carrying member of The Dead Club, will I turn too? Does he die when I die?

Do I die when he dies?

I need to make sure that I am taking good care of him. If I can feel pain when he feels pain, there is a strong chance that if something fatal happens to him that it will impact me too. I need to make sure that doesn't happen. Also, I don't want to see anything bad happen to him for his sake. I do care about the weird little sack of flour.

The Big Reveal

Mum, Vincent, and I moved into this house when I was a baby so my memories from that time of my life are basically made up from stories I've been told growing up. One of my favourite stories was one that mum told me about Crispy, the overweight agoraphobic dragon. I know that might sound like a strange bedtime fairytale, but according to mum, Crispy was real.

So the story goes, the reason mum was able to get this house for such a good price was because of Crispy. The house had been sitting on the market for years and although it had been viewed by dozens of potential buyers, no one wanted to buy a house that came with a large dragon occupying the basement who refused to leave. Crispy had no financial interest in the property, so was basically a giant green squatter.

What do you need to know about Crispy?

Crowded places must be avoided, it much prefers to isolate.

Risk of serious health problems due to its enormous weight.

If you scare the beast, it'll dispose of you like you were out of date.

Sleepy most of the time, for months on end, it will hibernate.

Painfully angry whenever someone tries to get it to vacate.

You won't last long when it's irate, one false move, and it's checkmate.

Mum had every intention of conversing with the dragon in an attempt to get it to withdraw from its underground dwelling. After the property contracts were exchanged and the keys were handed over, the moving van arrived to take us to our new home. Upon entering our lovely giant gothic mansion, there were no signs that a dragon was living there. In fact, the property didn't look lived in at all. It looked brand new but at the same time, a hundred years old. I understand what she meant by that now. The house is showing signs of what look like designed age. For example, there is a perfect crack down the kitchen wall that looks like it was surgically placed there by a team of skilled builders.

Once our possessions had been put away into their new homes, and us children were settled into our spooky but beautiful new bedrooms, mum decided to take a trip down into the basement to meet Crispy. She told me that as soon as she opened the basement door, she heard a distant groan of displeasure coming from deep within the dark space below. The basement is large, apparently large enough to house a fully grown, overweight dragon. Mum bravely descended the basement staircase, not knowing what to expect when she reached the bottom.

All she could see as she investigated the depths of the shadowy basement was a faint orange light not unlike a single candle atop a birthday cake. As she ventured further into the cavern, she said she could feel her temperature rising and that the faint flickering candlelight started to get brighter. She could now hear something breathing, and the sound was perfectly in sync with the flickering of the light which was growing stronger with every breath. She heard a deep booming voice shout to her from the darkness…

"GO AWAY!"

Mum said that she calmly tried to explain that she was a friend. That she had just moved into the house and that she wanted to help the dragon. She emphasised the fact that she was not there to hurt it.

The thundering voice came once again, this time even louder…

"GO AWAY"

I'm not sure if brave is the correct adjective to use for what she did next, but it's the word she used when she told me this story. Mum bravely stepped forward, ignoring the creature's warnings. The flickering light had graduated from a faint birthday cake candle to what looked like a very small, but very real forest fire.

Her next step finally revealed where the light was coming from - inside the dragon's mouth. From its position in the shadows of the basement, the dragon looked petrifying. The way it was positioned made it look like it was the size of the entire room, floor to ceiling. Before mum could open her mouth to speak again, the dragon's head lurched forward, and with one breath, it set the whole room ablaze.

Mum told me that she remembered seeing a blinding white light as the flames approached her. She thought her life had come to an end when she felt the scorching heat of the inferno surrounding her. She opened her eyes and saw that the flames were all around her, but miraculously not touching her. If she had moved a hand in any direction a fraction of an inch, she would have been engulfed. The dragon's flames came pouring out for what felt like an age, but not a single ember touched her. When the fire eventually died down, it became clear that this had merely been a warning from the dragon. The walls of the basement were scorched black, and the room was filled with smoke.

As the smoke started to clear, mum stepped forward once again and laid eyes upon the dragon for the first time. Although she was shocked by what she saw, the word she used to describe what stood in front of her was 'underwhelming'. Based on the stories she had been told, the monstrous voice she had heard and the near-death experience she had just encountered, she was expecting something quite different. In her mind she had pictured a giant and formidable beast but instead, what stood in front of her was a rather pathetic looking plump dragon who was so out of breath she thought it was about to collapse.

What came next was a very interesting interaction which I will attempt to transcribe from my memory for you…

```
INT. The Basement. Dusk.
Crispy the dragon is struggling to catch its breath after
breathing fire for the first time in years. The action
has clearly taken a lot out of the creature. Edward's mum
approaches it with her hands up in a sign of peace.
```

Mum: Are you ok?
Crispy: Yes…
Mum: What's your name?
Crispy: Leave me alone.

The dragon slowly catches its breath. Edward's mum takes one final step towards it and places a hand on its scaly back.

Mum: I'm not here to hurt you.
Crispy: You wish for me to leave this house.
Mum: No, not if you don't want to.
Crispy: You will let me stay?
Mum: Yes. I want you to stay.

From that moment on, the two of them grew a mightily strong friendship.

To be honest, I never really thought that this story was true when I was little. It's only been the last few years since The War and Frank's strange and peculiar existence that I have started to really think about the possibility of this story being true.

Depending on whether I was still awake or not, sometimes the bedtime story of Crispy would continue, and mum would explain how the dragon came to reside in our basement, and why it was so reluctant to leave. Mum told me that Crispy suffered with agoraphobia, meaning it had a crippling fear of leaving the house in case it found itself in open and crowded spaces. Allegedly, the dragon had eaten an entire year's worth of food in an attempt to hibernate in the solitude of this empty house. This would certainly explain why the dragon was so portly. It had managed to hibernate for all of six days before it woke up, starving hungry. I'm told that the first thing the dragon did once mum gained its trust was ask her to order it a pizza.

It's implausible details like this that made the story too ridiculous to believe.

Mum told me that she would put me and Vincent down to sleep in the evenings and then go down to the basement and sit with Crispy for hours, just talking to it. She named the dragon Crispy after multiple failed attempts to find out its name, only to be greeted by abject confusion. A bit like every time I ask Frank a question of any category. After a while, Crispy opened up to her about its irrational fear of leaving the house. Mum listened to the dragon's concerns and explained that it had nothing to fear, and that if it wanted to stay here in the basement, it could stay for as long as liked.

It was close to a year of conversations between mum and the dragon that ultimately led to Crispy not only losing weight, but also believing that it was once again brave enough to leave the house and take to the skies. The dragon felt more alert, stronger, and more powerful than ever before, but it was still in the basement. However, the reason it didn't want to leave had now changed. It was no longer because of fear of the outside, it was because it didn't want to leave my mum. Crispy had enjoyed their conversations and being fed healthy, albeit green food. It had enjoyed being looked after. That being said, it also knew that it couldn't stay down in the basement forever.

I only remember hearing mum tell the true ending of this tale once. It must have been because I refused to go to sleep, because the longer I stayed up, the more of the story I got to hear. So, there is a chance that the end of this story is a genuine memory, but there is also a chance that it's come from a dream.

Mum told me that Crispy wanted to thank her for everything she had done. Although the dragon had no possessions to present her with, no way of paying her back for the food or her time. The one thing it did have though was a handful of dragon scales. Mum made these things sound magical, but all I can picture is a dragon peeling what I imagine looked like scabs off of its back and then handing them over to her. Crispy said that these scales contained a magical power that with time, she would be able to wield herself. To this day, this is still the only possible explanation I have for the existence of Frank and the other creatures that roam this house. Although, something about it still doesn't ring true to me.

I think that one of the following three outcomes could be true:

1. Crispy the dragon was nothing more than a bedtime story that my mum used to tell me to help me get to sleep. I believe that this is the most likely.

2. Crispy the dragon was real, and despite mum's description that it was a giant creature, it was somehow small enough to fit in and out of the basement door, as this is the only entrance and exit.

3. Crispy the dragon is real and is somehow still down in that basement.

I have more questions about this Crispy the dragon story that I would like to get answers to. Unfortunately, I don't have anyone left that could ask, so all I can do is write down my theories here, knowing full well that they will never be explained.

If Crispy was the magnificent beast that has been described, how did it get into that basement without bringing the whole house down? How did it manage to control the fire to ensure mum wasn't burned? If it's still in the basement, why haven't I seen or heard from it? If the dragon is still down there, what's it eating?

There is no way this is anything more than a fairytale. I really wish the third option is true. I wish that Crispy is real. A dragon would be extremely useful in an apocalypse. However, this would also mean that if there is a magical, invisible dragon in the basement right now, it's sharing the space with Spike.

INTER
MISSION

Intermission

I thought I'd step away from everything and stretch my legs for a bit. Some of these memories are quite painful to dig up and relive on the page. Then again, so are some of the more recent events that I've recorded on these pages. An example occurred just before bed last night. Frank wanted to discover if he could fly by jumping from the top step of the third-floor staircase. Again. I didn't see him do it, but I certainly felt it when he bashed his head on the stairs just seconds after takeoff. I also felt the succeeding blows to the head and body as he bounced down not only the entirety of the third-floor staircase, but the second-floor staircase as well. Amazing, considering he would've had to get up and walk across the hallway before he reached the top of the second staircase. Unsurprisingly, I felt a little lightheaded after that, so I decided not to go straight to bed for fear of concussion. I thought I'd stay up and have a drink.

I never tasted alcohol before The War. I was too young for mum to let me sample it, and I never tried to sneak any behind her back.

There is a small drinks cabinet that she used to refer to as the bar. Not too long into my self-imposed lockdown, I decided to take inventory of all the food and drink in the house. Once I had accounted for everything in the pantry and what was left in the kitchen, I remembered about the bar. I found quite a few half empty bottles and a handful of full ones too. As I started removing the bottles to see just how many there were, I came across something else. Amongst the bottles of old whisky and rum, was a little garden gnome dressed like a bartender. He was wearing a tiny bow tie, and had a white towel draped over his arm and what appeared to be a cork for a hat.

Mum was never a big drinker, but there was the odd occasion when I could tell she was feeling low, and she would have a 'medicinal' drink. She would be fine and then all of a sudden, she would pause, look deep in thought, and then look completely different. Anything that reminded her of Vincent would bring on this reaction. She usually did a stellar job of hiding her emotions from me. For example, if she was feeling low and wanted a little drink to take the edge off, she wouldn't just grab a bottle from the bar and disappear into her bedroom for hours. Instead, she would perform a magic trick for me. She would sit me down on the floor in the dining room and shout out her drink order to no one other than the room itself. Then, she would slowly walk towards the bar, all the while keeping her eyes fixed on mine. Then, out of nowhere, we would hear the sound of a tiny bell ringing from inside the bar, signally that her order was ready. When she opened the lid of the drinks cabinet, her drink would be sitting there waiting for her, as if by magic. She'd pick it up and present it like it was the payoff to some elaborate stage magic act. I would laugh and never question how the feat was achieved.

Well, it turns out that it was a little bartending gnome hanging out in the bar, fixing the drinks for her all along. Although this was an entirely different type of magic, it still took away some of the shine when I finally saw how the trick was accomplished. Sometimes it's better not to peek behind the curtain.

Laying eyes on the bar gnome for the first time was a surreal experience. He stepped forward and began a rather strange conversation with me...

INT. The Dining Room. Late afternoon.
Gork, the bar gnome is standing on the edge of the drinks cabinet looking up at Edward with an expressionless look on his face.

Gork: Language?
Edward: Sorry?
Gork: What do you want my default language to be?
Edward: I don't know. English?
Gork: Confirmed. Do you want me to connect to the Wi-Fi?
Edward: What? What do you mean?
Gork: If I connect to the Wi-Fi, I can download new cocktail recipes for you. Would you like to connect now, or do this later?
Edward: Err, later.
Gork: Confirmed. Would you like to create a new user profile or login to an existing account?
Edward: Umm, I really don't know what's happening.
Gork: Would you like to skip this step for now?
Edward: Yes, please.
Gork: Would you like to turn on notifications?

Edward: `Look, I really don't understand what is going on. Why are you asking me all these questions?`

It turned out that the gnome was some sort of bar butler. His sole purpose was to mix drinks at his owner's request. Since mum was no longer around and she'd been the only previous user, the gnome recognised me as a potential new user and was going through his initial setup phase with me. He gave me a rather large user manual to peruse which explained everything in perfect detail. Trust me, any bizarre questions you might have right now are answered somewhere in the six-hundred-page instruction booklet.

Towards the end of the booklet, there were some example commands that you could give the bar gnome, as well as a few cocktail recipes. At the back of the book was a notes section designed to be a blank space for you to write down your own drink recipes. It brought a smile to my face to see my mum's handwriting in the book. She had only been gone for a few weeks at this point, but I was missing her so much. I read through the cocktail recipe she had written and saw it was the only one she'd added.

The Chocolate Orange
Bourbon - 50ml
Chocolate Liqueur - 20ml
Sugar Syrup - 20ml
Orange Bitters - 4 dashes
(Mix in the glass and serve with ice)

The bar gnome was standing and staring expectantly at me while I read the recipe. Without giving too much thought to the consequences, I asked him to make the cocktail that my mum had invented. The tiny butler disappeared into the back of the bar and started working immediately. Moments later he rang a very small bell to indicate that the task had been completed. Then, it was time to take my very first taste of alcohol.

It was very strong and although I could appreciate the overall sweetness of the drink, my main tasting note was definitely 'fire'. The drink burned out my mouth, and the searing feeling of fire continued down my throat and into my stomach. To be honest, it made me feel pretty sick for a while afterwards.

I certainly haven't made a habit of drinking since my discovery of the bar gnome, but I do pop in and see him every now and again. It's quite refreshing to see a garden gnome that isn't trying to kill me, unlike the one that lives in the garden. I did try to add a non-alcoholic drink to the blank space at the back of the book, but the bar gnome refused to make it. He said it had to contain an amount of alcohol in order for him to make it, as he is not programmed to make mocktails. I've since amended the beverage to include alcohol, just to give me a reason to visit the little mixologist. So last night, even though I was pretty certain I didn't have a concussion, it was a good excuse to spend some time at the bar.

The Blackcurrant Sour
Blackcurrant Squash - 50ml
H2O - 100ml
Sugar Syrup - 5ml
Bourbon - As little as possible please
(Pour it into a cup. Thanks)

Popcorn

Before the world ended, I used to eat a lot of rubbish food. I was a very fussy eater growing up. My perfect Sunday dinner was roast potatoes and salt. My old rule would have been *'if it isn't potato in the form of a smiley face, or breaded turkey shaped like a dinosaur, I'm not eating it'*. Believe it or not, that kind of thinking isn't going to help your chances of survival, apocalypse or not.

Survival Rule #3 - Eat Healthy

You need to keep your strength up by eating healthy. The less you enjoy your food, the better it is for you.

Since being locked down, my attitude has changed drastically. Before, the only green food I ate was apple flavoured gummy sweets. Now, I eat every type of vegetable there is. Do I enjoy them? Of course not, but it's my only option.

We don't have a farm and we don't have an endless supply of tinned food, and we don't have a golden goose that lays chocolate eggs. Although, thinking about it, that last one is probably the most likely one that I would stumble across in this house.

Alas, despite the strange things that live within these walls, there is no magic supply of food. The pantry is running out quickly so now if it doesn't grow in the garden, I don't eat it. I know I can survive on the food in the garden. I know I can live a long and healthy life on that diet. Just as long as I stay clear of the undead garden gnome.

I still miss the lovely food I used to eat though. The thing I miss the most are large tubs of salted popcorn, drowning in delicious pools of hot melted butter that I would get every time I went to the cinema.

Flashback

I've been thinking about a day that took place a few months before The War started. Looking back, I think it was the best day of my life. I didn't think that at the time though. Looking back, it was just another ordinary day. Nothing particularly special happened, but when I think back on all my memories before The War started, this is my favourite. Something about it just really stands out in my mind. Maybe it's because it was one of the last times I felt truly happy.

It was a Saturday, my friend Victoria and her mum were coming over to our house for the afternoon. Victoria's mum and my mum worked together and were good friends. Despite my thinly veiled protests, we were going to be baking. I didn't really mind; I knew it would be fun. I thought that the 'manly' thing to do was to at least pretend to object so that it didn't seem like I was actually looking forward to it. Spending time with Victoria was always so much fun though.

I still don't know why this memory has stayed with me. We weren't doing anything exciting, just talking and listening to music while we baked little gingerbread men. At one point, Victoria asked to see some of mum's experiments; she was always obsessed with them. Mum started to show us some of the projects she had been working on in her spare time when she got a phone call. She said the call was from the office and that it was an emergency. She never got calls on a weekend. Then, she and Victoria's mum had to leave in a hurry, so Victoria and I were left to finish the baking alone. I never did find out why mum had to go into the office that day. She never mentioned it again.

The oven opened with a smell like heaven,
The gingerbread men came out,
Of which there were eleven.
They were all big, tall and strong,
Apart from the little one in the corner,
He was just all wrong.
His body was so small,
He looked nothing like his brothers,
Nothing like them at all.
He was too scrawny and thin,
No one wanted to eat him,
So he was just thrown in the bin.

The baking went quite well, and the gingerbread men tasted pretty good for the most part. Victoria said she would stay with me until our mum's got back, even though she could have gone home to see her dad. I don't think she really got on well with him. I was more than happy for her to stay. I showed her my video games and we sat in the Den and played for hours.

I've been thinking about scripting one of our conversations but nothing overly profound was said. In fact, we sat in silence for most of the time, but it was lovely. Something about it just made me feel so happy. I would give anything to go back to that moment again.

About a week after The War started, I found myself struggling to change the bin liner in the kitchen (due to my cack-hands). As I lifted the full bag out, I noticed something lying at the bottom of the bin. It was one of the gingerbread men that we'd made that day. It was the little one that didn't come out right, the one we discarded. It was lying there looking very sad and helpless. As I bent down to pick him up, I noticed he was grimacing like he was in pain. I suddenly thought about that day we made him and how happy I was. As I stood there daydreaming, Frank took the gingerbread man out of my hand and started eating him.

I thought about Victoria and wondered how she was coping with this lockdown. All week I had been telling myself the same thing, that she must be safe.

I then started to think, what if she's not?

Right then and there I decided that I had to do something. I had to know if she was safe or not. The only way I was going to find out would be to leave the house.

ACT III

Act III - Damsel in Distress

This is my reckoning of the week after The War began, and the last time I left the house.

At this point, it had been over a week since my long day of standing by the window and watching the world slowly come to an end through a telescope. Every day since, I had been thinking about the same thing, was Victoria OK? I had to find out. But every time I thought about opening the front door, I'd see something outside that made me panic and change my mind. The previous evening, I had my bag packed with supplies and was just about to open the front door when I heard a scream coming from outside. By the time I made it to the living room window, all I could see was a horde of the Dead, freshly fed and walking down the street leaving a mangled carcass of a human behind them. I dropped my bag on the floor and went straight up to bed, hating myself for not being brave enough. My alarm clock woke me up at 8 o'clock the next morning and I told myself that no matter what I saw outside my window today, I would leave the house. No matter what.

I couldn't tell Frank what I was doing because he would just try and stop me again. He wouldn't understand if I explained it to him and even if he did, knowing him the way I do now, he would've probably wanted to come with me. Instead of attempting to explain my plan to this creepy little voodoo doll that I had barely spoken to, and the reasons why he wouldn't be able to accompany me, I instead decided to ask him to play a game of hide and seek with me. This has since become my 'break glass in case of emergency' move when Frank gets too much for me. He always hides in the same place and stays there for hours if I don't come and find him. I appreciate its quite cruel, but it works so well. It doesn't hurt him, and I don't do it all the time. Honestly.

With the weird voodoo doll off in his hiding place, I grabbed my supply bag and baseball bat, then walked directly to the front door without looking back. I knew that if I had looked out of the window first there was a strong chance that I'd see something that would put me off going out there. This was the only way. I half closed my eyes as I walked through the doorway, and quickly closed the door behind me. As I opened my eyes, I feared what I was about to see.

To my surprise, there was no one out there. No dead people. No living people. No one. I didn't hear any screaming or any sirens. Nothing. It actually looked quite peaceful out there. I took a step forward and heard a noise. It sounded like someone repeatedly and uncontrollably shouting the word "balls", like a bad cough. The voice belonged to Larry, the gargoyle. I'd forgotten that he was up there. The violent coughing of the words continued, and for a moment I completely forgot what I was doing out there.

EXT. The Porch. Morning.
Edward is standing nervously holding a black steel baseball bat. He slowly steps forward and looks up at the roof of the house.

Edward: Are you OK Larry?
Larry: Aye. BALLS! Sorry. Whit ye daein'?
Edward: I'm going to find my friend. I need to make sure that she's alright.
Larry: Dinnae gang oot thare. Tis nae safe.
Edward: I have to, I have to know.
Larry: Yer mam wanted ye 'ere.
Edward: I know, but mums not here is she.
Larry: She's comin' back ye ken.
Edward: No, I don't know that. I wish I did.

I decided to ignore the gargoyle's advice and set out on what I hoped would be a nice short journey. Victoria's house was only around the corner, so the round trip should've only taken a few minutes. I knew my estimated time of arrival back home would be completely dependent on what I found when I arrived at her house. I honestly didn't know what to expect.

I reached the end of my driveway and paused. Never in my life had looking both ways before I crossed the street been more important. I still couldn't see anything to be concerned about. Sure, the burnt-out car in the middle of the road was a bit grim and the pools of blood scattered every five yards where a person had lost their life weren't the most cheerful sights to see, but the point was that there was no immediate danger. I cautiously began walking down the street.

Every other house on my road looked abandoned. The front doors were wide open, the windows were smashed and had blood stains around the broken glass. Had it really only been a week? The houses that didn't look abandoned still didn't show any signs of life. If anyone was living in them, they certainly weren't standing at their windows and waving. I could see the end of my street where the road forked. Turning left would take me on the path towards the city centre, the last place I wanted to be. I needed to turn right. As soon as I made that turn, I would be able to see Victoria's house.

The last house before the fork in the road belonged to Mrs. Jones. Something laying in front of the driveway of her house caught my attention. As I moved closer towards it, my fears were confirmed. Mrs. Jones had a little dog. He was a nervous little thing but incredibly loyal to her and never left her side. I never knew what the dog's name was but the little tag on the collar of what remained of him said 'Chip'. One look up at the driveway towards the house told me everything I needed to know about what happened to Mrs. Jones and Chip. It wouldn't be a pleasant tale to recount in these pages. Not that the tale I'm telling is particularly pleasant either.

As I stood there piecing together what must have happened, I heard a noise off in the distance, behind me. It's funny, because the first thing that noise made me think about was that the movies had got it all wrong. How many zombie movies have you seen where the protagonist is in a quiet, dark room and the zombie manages to sneak up on them without making a sound? It's ludicrous. The Dead make so much noise, they are incapable of staying quiet.

The dead man making the noise was far away enough not to have noticed me yet. I had time to move. I knew this was bound to happen at some point, and I was prepared. Although I had my baseball bat in hand, I decided that using it would be my last resort. My first port of call would be to run and hide. I had spent the whole week watching people fight these things through my telescope and the order of play was almost always the same:

- The living would take on one of the Dead.
- They would make enough noise to attract more of them.
- More of the Dead would come.
- They would fight them too.
- More noise was made.
- More of the Dead came.
- This process would be repeated until the living were outnumbered.
- The living joins The Dead Club.

It didn't matter what weapons they had or how many were in their group, the Dead always won. The only people who managed to get away were the ones who ran and hid until the Dead left. In my mind, I called "Action" and my feet started to move in the direction I asked them to go.

Survival Rule #4 - Stay Hidden

Hide first, fight second. Anytime there is the opportunity to stay hidden out of sight, choose to stay there for as long as you can.

I quickly ducked behind the bushes in Mrs. Jones' front garden and lay down flat on the grass to make sure there was no way the dead man could see me. I could just about see him through the gaps in the bushes. I just had to stay hidden until he passed by. The good news was that he hadn't seen me and was continuing on his original path. The bad news was that his original path was leading directly to Victoria's street.

The dead man looked familiar, but I couldn't work out why. Just as his face was about to move into focus, I heard a noise. The noise wasn't coming from the dead man, this was a new noise. This new noise was a much more pained moan, and it was coming from the opposite direction to the dead man. The new noise was coming from what remained of Mrs. Jones's half eaten mutilated body, and it was slowly crawling towards me. Half of her face was missing where it had been eaten, one of her arms had been torn off and her torso looked like a half-eaten pie without any of the filling left inside. Her entire lower half must have been somewhere else in the garden because it wasn't attached to what was left of her torso anymore. Her one remaining hand reached out in front of her, and her fingers dug into the earth, pulling herself forward in what looked like agonising pain. Except the Dead don't feel pain. The blood lust alone was enough to pull her forward. It was a horrible sight to behold, the rotting corpse of an old woman torn in half, clawing herself towards me.

I looked back through the bushes and saw that the dead man was closer now. He was still moving in the same direction, but if I were to stand up and move now, I would definitely be seen. My gaze moved back to Mrs. Jones's corpse crawling, who had inched closer and who's moans were getting louder as the distance between us closed. I was trapped, and the walls were closing in on me slowly. I had to make a decision, I had to act.

My options were either to kill the crawler and potentially alert the walker, or stand up and attempt to kill the walker and potentially alert more of the Dead. Before I had a chance to weigh up the options, Mrs. Jones had become dangerously close. I quietly shuffled myself into a position where I could swing my bat, forgetting to check behind me to see how close the dead man was. I didn't want to do it; I didn't want to kill her. But I had no choice. She was here now.

I swung my bat at the old woman's head, which burst open, exploding like a watermelon. All those years of watching films and playing video games hadn't desensitised me like people said it would. When I saw that head explode, I felt a sickness in my stomach like I'd never felt before. Even though I knew it wasn't really Mrs. Jones that I killed, I still felt horribly guilty. She was the first dead one that I put down myself. Something told me that she probably wouldn't be the last. There wasn't any time to think too seriously about what had just happened as I needed to check on the whereabouts of the walking dead man behind me. There would be time to process my impossibly difficult emotions later.

The dead man's path had changed. He must have heard the noise because he was now staggering at pace towards the bushes. I could see his face now and it finally dawned on me who he was. The dead man was Victoria's father, or at least his poorly reanimated corpse. My mind raced with questions. If he was out here, did it mean Victoria would be too? Would I find her wandering these streets somewhere? All I could do was hold my breath and stay as still as possible. I could see his feet on the other side of the bushes. A small hole in one of his shoes was leaking blood that was pooling around him as he stood eerily still, looking for whatever had made that melon bursting noise a moment ago. The sound of his groaning voice felt deafening at this close proximity. I could hear his body leaning against the fragile bushes. If he pushed forward, he would fall right on top of me. I would have to stand and fight him before that happened. I've always thought of myself as a child, which is why I always thought I could never get hurt. When I was young, I thought that nothing bad would ever happen to me. Bad things happened to adults, not children. My brother's disappearance admittedly burst that bubble, but being out here has completely destroyed the theory. Being outside and face to face with the Dead, it doesn't matter who you are. No one is safe. Bad things can happen to anyone.

Just as I was about to finally take a much needed gulp of air and stand up, something made the dead man move away. Maybe he heard something, maybe his internal script told him to keep moving in the direction he was originally headed. On reflection, I have started to wonder if there was any part of the man that he used to be in there somewhere. Maybe he was trying to go home? Thoughts like that don't help me sleep at night, especially when I think about Mrs. Jones and how I exploded her old watermelon head.

I remained hidden in those bushes for as long as I could. I sat and waited for my heart rate to return to a manageable 100 beats per minute, then quietly rose to my feet and continued my quest.

I finally made it to the fork in the road, my first checkpoint. Looking down the road to the left I could just about see the giant purple mosh pit that was the city centre. To the right, I could see Victoria's street which looked quiet. There was no sign of her dad. I must have waited long enough for him to stagger away. I slowly made my way along the street without interruption. This street was even worse than mine. Every house looked abandoned; some had even burnt down. I tried not to think about how unlikely it was that I would find Victoria alive, given what I had seen so far out there. I kept going because I still had to know for sure. One way or the other.

Victoria's house was finally in front of me. From where I was standing the house still looked pretty good. I could only see the top half because of the tall hedges that surrounded the boundary of the property, but the part that I could see looked untouched. There were no signs of broken glass or fire. It looked the same as it did the last time I saw it, just over a week ago. I could even see Victoria's bedroom window from where I stood. I knew it was hers because of the picture she had painted in the window. It was of two angel wings forming the shape of a love heart. The sight of that picture filled me with a feeling I wasn't sure I would ever feel again.

I made my way to the opening in the hedges which led to the front door. As I walked through the archway, I saw something I wasn't expecting, something I really hoped I wouldn't see. The bottom half of the house that had remained hidden by the hedges looked perfect, no broken windows, the front door was shut and there were no signs of bodies on the floor. The thing I didn't want to see was Victoria's dead dad stood perfectly still, looking up at the house.

I had been so slow and cautious up until this point, but the adrenaline surging through my body made me turn that corner at such a pace that I almost bumped into the standing corpse. The scuff of my shoes abruptly stopping and stepping backwards on instinct was enough to alert the dead man, who looked a lot bigger than I remembered. He slowly turned and saw me. His eyes expanded, almost doubling in size, and a look of pure rage fixed on his face. He made that unbearable screaming sound, the one that pierces through you like a needle being plunged into your ears. What happened next was a complete blur at the time and probably all took place in a matter of seconds:

I took a step backwards.
I saw a figure in the window of the house behind Victoria's dad.
I heard a noise coming from the street behind me.
I turned around and ran back through the archway.
I looked back to see that Victoria's dad had started walking towards me.

As soon as I stepped into the archway I was trapped. There were three more of the Dead staggering towards me that must have seen me walk into the house because they were already approaching at a frightening pace. I looked back, trying to decide which direction would provide the best chance of survival. The figure at the window was now clear to me from this angle. It was Victoria. She was alive.

I had no time to process this information as her dead dad was nearly on me. My instincts took me through the archway towards the three dead people. These were three more faces that I will never forget. I recognised one of them as Victoria's mum. I knew her well when she was alive. She and my mum were good friends and colleagues, and I think it was because of their friendship that Victoria and I became such good friends. With both of Victoria's parents dead, did that mean that she was on her own in that house? How long had she been in there? These questions flashed in my mind for less than a second. By the looks of Victoria's mum, she hadn't been dead for very long. None of her skin was rotting and she was moving quite ably.

The second dead person was very different and not someone I recognised. He looked like he had been dead for a very long time. I know it could have only been a week at this point, but he looked like a skeleton that someone had poorly attached some muscles and the odd bit of loose skin to.

The third member of The Dead Club was only a child, and could only have been about eight years old. His head was leaning to one side and his neck appeared to have some chunks missing from it. He was also missing most of his left arm and a part of his skull, leaving his brain exposed to the elements. The child was unrecognisable. He could have been someone that I had seen every day of my life. But in his current form, I don't think his own parents would have been able to identify him.

The mother, the skeleton and the child were all walking towards me at different speeds with the mother being the closest. I pulled back my bat and swung it as hard as I could, but I miscalculated the distance. I missed the brain and hit her in the jaw instead, which was taken clean off. The force of the hit knocked her backwards onto the ground and into the path of the skeleton, but it had also spun me round so that I was face to face with Victoria's dad again. I didn't have the space or the time to take a swing at him. All I could manage was a heavy jab with the bat to keep him away from me. The jab bought me enough space to take a swing, but I couldn't generate enough power to put him down. The bat connected with the side of his head and did some serious damage to both his skull and to my bat, which was now dripping with thick, red blood. Some of the black paint on the bat had been scratched off, revealing the steel beneath, and there were three small chrome lines, like claw marks, now on the top of the bat.

Before I could attempt a second shot, I sensed the presence of the child behind me as he reached out for me with his remaining arm. I managed to kick him back and deliver a two-handed swing down on top of his head. The vibrations from the hit felt like an electric shock. The bat was lodged in the child's skull and the blood from the fatal blow covered me like some sort of evil ice bucket challenge. I dropped the bat and attempted to scoop the treacle like goo from my face when I heard a sound that broke my heart…

"Edward!"

The desperate cry could only be coming from one place, not that I could see it. I opened my eyes to see Victoria's dad right in front of me. The sound of the scream had stolen his attention and he was turning back towards the house. As I attempted to look past him, my eyes searching for the source of the shout, the skeleton lunged at me from behind. I twisted my shoulder at the last second and narrowly avoided his grasp. He stumbled forward and fell to the ground in front of me. This earned me a second of respite to finally look up at the house. I saw Victoria standing at the open doorway. She was holding a pot in one hand, a frying pan in the other and was frantically banging them together. She was doing everything she could to get the dead man away from me and focus their murderous hunger towards her instead. Before I could open my mouth to say a word, she beat me to it…

"Behind you!"

Victoria's mother had regained her composure, now completely separated from her bottom jaw. Even though she was probably no longer able to successfully bite me, this didn't stop her from trying to and didn't make her seem like any less of a threat. I didn't have my bat as it was still taking residence in the child's defunct brain, so my only choice was to fight her off with my bare hands. I reached up and grabbed her by the shoulders like a wrestler and then immediately realised I had no idea what I was doing. She was so strong, much stronger than she looked. It took everything I had to keep her horrific half a face away from mine.

As we grappled and spun around, I managed to glance to the left and the right of her. To the left, I could see the skeleton struggling to get back up on his feet, and to the right I could see Victoria's father getting closer to his daughter as she continued to bang her kitchenware together as loudly as possible.

My vocabulary was failing me almost as much as the strength in my arms. All I could muster up was the word **"No!"** to summarise the situation. I didn't want to be here. This isn't what I wanted to happen. I wanted to save my friend, not put her in danger. As much as I tried, I couldn't shake the dead woman off and now the skeleton was back up and making his way over to us. I edged backwards to create some distance between us and the skeleton. The banging noise had stopped, so I tried to take a look at the house once more and saw that Victoria was still standing in the doorway, only now she was holding a kitchen knife. Why wasn't she closing the door? Her dad was almost there. Why was she standing right there? He was about to get her. It's because of me. She's trying to save me just like I'm trying to save her. I was failing. I took my eyes off the immediate threat in front of me for too long, and I was made to pay the price. Victoria's mother pushed me back and I stumbled to the ground with her on top of me. Blood dripped from her permanently open mouth and onto my face. The skeleton followed us down like an elderly relative on a twister mat. And then I heard it. I couldn't see what was happening, I didn't need to.

Victoria screamed.

I suddenly felt a blast of superhuman strength like those mothers you hear about who can lift cars over their heads when their children are in danger. I released my right hand and used it to lift this mother's head clean off of her shoulders. Now I could see three things.

The first thing I saw directly in front of me was the skeleton who had taken the mother's place on top of me. The second thing was the horde of at least twenty of the Dead approaching from down the street. The third was Victoria.

I could only see flashes of her as I struggled with the skeleton. I saw Victoria's dad falling on top of her. I heard the vicious skeleton on top of me as well as the horde of the approaching corpses gaining speed, but those sounds faded away when I heard Victoria's scream as she fell, and the way it instantly stopped when she hit the ground.

As tears filled my eyes and emptiness filled my heart, I hit the skeleton as hard as I could and stole one last glimpse at my friend as she lay perfectly still while her dad successfully made sure that every single member of his household became a fully-fledged member of The Dead Club.

As my view became obscured once more, I felt a plague of unbearable emotions befall me. Part of me wanted to lie still and let it all come to end, but the other part was pure rage. The superhuman strength was nothing compared to the power of fury mode. I grabbed the skeleton by the neck and pulled his head down towards the concrete. The monster groaned, still showing signs of life even in death, so I slammed his head down again. And again. And again, until all I could see was the red mist of hate and anger. I knew the horde was getting closer, but I just kept smashing what was left of this disgusting thing in my hands on the ground outside my best friend's house. My best friend who was dead because of me.

I should have got up and tried to stop Victoria's dad from eating her. I should have at least done that for her. I should have wrenched my bat from the dead child's skull and used it to avenge my friend. But I didn't. I just kept hitting this skeleton into the ground until all I was holding onto was a piece of bone connected to a broken spine. I looked up to see that the horde was only a few steps away from me now and closed my eyes.

It had all been for nothing. If I'd just stayed at home, she would be OK. If I'd been brave enough to get to her sooner, I might have been able to save her. She risked her life for me. She gave her life for mine. I couldn't allow that to be for nothing. I opened my eyes.

As much as the rage and sadness inside me wanted to pick up that bat and bash Victoria's dad's head in until there was nothing left, I knew that I'd be trapped if I did. Instead, I stood up and decided not to look back at the house. I couldn't bear to see what he was doing to her. I ran away as fast as I could, leaving the horde behind me. I ran past her mother's decapitated but still moving head. I ran back around the corner, passing Mrs. Jones and poor little Chip's remains. I kept running until I was outside my front door. I looked back just in time to see the leader of horde turn the corner. I darted inside quickly, in the hope that it hadn't seen me. Today had been a bad day.

I locked the front door behind me. Frank was still in his hiding place, lying face down underneath a coffee table in the living room. At least, his head was under the coffee table, his plump body, arms, and legs were all sticking out in plain sight. I didn't want to speak to him. I just climbed up the stairs and went into my bedroom. I closed the door and crawled into bed with no intention of ever coming out again. I cried myself to sleep that night, and every night that week. I had an overwhelming feeling of anxious sickness that I couldn't get rid of. The feeling of dread filled me every waking hour. I tried to sleep for as long as I could so I could stop thinking about what had happened. This is when the bad dreams started. Now everyone I cared about was gone.

It's all my fault. I'm the reason I'm alone.

The next few days were a blur. I couldn't eat anything. I didn't want to. I don't remember much about that period. I know that I got pretty sick. I remember Frank would stand outside my bedroom door because I heard him knocking daily. I think some people might have tried to get into the house at one point because I heard banging on the front door downstairs. I couldn't muster any strength to get up though. I had stopped caring. Outside Victoria's house I told myself I had to stay alive otherwise her sacrifice was for nothing, but that feeling drifted away and had been replaced by an unbearable weight of sadness. I could barely lift my own head from the pillow. I got to the stage where I just didn't want to exist anymore. It was at my absolute lowest when I decided I couldn't go on anymore. I got out of bed for the first time in days and went to the bedroom door. When I opened it, Frank was standing there, looking up at me.

INT. Outside Edward's bedroom. Time of day unknown.
Edward is standing in the same clothes he has been wearing for the last several days. Frank doesn't wear clothes. Frank looks up at Edward with giant unblinking eyes.

Frank: You didn't come and find me.

Pause.

Edward smiles as his eyes fill with tears. He slowly gets down onto his knees and hugs the voodoo doll.

Edward: I'm so sorry.

The next day, Frank helped me break down the garden shed and some old wooden furniture to make boards for all the doors and windows. He wasn't much help, but the thought was there. We started the long process of making the house a fortress. I decided that I wouldn't be going outside again. Not until this was all over. That feels like such a long time ago now. It still isn't over.

Deleted Scene

Pickup Shots

I haven't picked up this diary for a while. It's been a few months since I wrote those pages about Victoria's death, and I think it really took it out of me. I don't think I have processed the emotions properly yet. Reliving that day sent me into a bit of a depression spiral and I really didn't feel like writing anything anymore. I put the diary in my bedside drawer with no intention of taking it out again.

This morning I woke up with a strange sensation I have never experienced before. I am normally jolted awake by my nightmares, but today was different. It wasn't a sound that woke me, and it wasn't something in my subconscious telling me to get up. It was a feeling in my mouth, which I appreciate sounds a bit odd. My lips felt warm, like they were pressed against a mug of hot coffee. I opened my eyes and saw that Frank was standing on top of my bedside table, his mouth wide open and his lips wrapped around the light bulb of my bedside lamp. I'd fallen asleep with the lamp on last night so needless to say, the bulb was very hot. Why Frank felt the need to 'taste' the red-hot bulb is a question I won't ever be able to answer. I quickly pushed him off the table, which then toppled over. The diary fell out onto the floor, along with my now broken bedside lamp.

Seeing the diary lying there on the floor got me thinking about Victoria, Vincent, and my mum. Not in a melancholy way, but just in terms of their stories. I honestly don't know at this point if there is anyone alive out there, so I don't know if there is anyone left to remember them, but I do. As long as I'm alive and have my memories, it's almost like they're all still alive too. My brother taught me that. I suddenly realised what my mum meant when she said that the meaning of life was 'Love, Dream, Create'. I know I won't ever be a father, I won't ever get to see my life story in a film on the big screen, but I can create a legacy in another way. I can write down our stories in an attempt to keep their memories alive.

I am also going to start barricading my bedroom door at night so that Frank can't get in here. My mouth is still burning.

Freeze Frame

It's snowing outside today, for the first time since the year The War started. I lost track of time a while ago, but I do remember the first winter and the first Christmas after the world ended. I remember sitting by the telescope on the third floor and watching the snow fall all over all the destruction and death. Overnight, it had all been blanketed with a beautiful bed of snow and at first glance, the world looked like it had returned to normal. The War started on April 2nd, so it had been around eight months by this point. I still had a basic idea what time of year it was. It would have been my favourite time of year.

Christmas was always such a special time for me when I was little. Mum would make such an effort to ensure it was a magical time for us, and Vincent played along for my sake even after he had clearly outgrown it. I remember coming down the stairs on Christmas morning to find a note under the Christmas tree. Santa wouldn't just leave us presents under the tree that we could rip open and immediately forget about. Instead, Vincent and I would be left clues to solve in order to find our gifts. There would be an envelope marked with the number one under the tree each year, and inside was a clue to where we could find the second envelope. The envelopes would be hidden all over the house in different locations. Sometimes they would include a riddle for us to solve, sometimes there would be a challenge we had to complete before the whereabouts of the next envelope was revealed, and sometimes there would even be little presents hidden along the way. The last envelope would have a star symbol on it instead of a number, and inside it would tell us where to find our main present.

I know now that this was mum's way of making the day last longer and stretching out the presents. She didn't have a lot of money and wasn't able to afford to buy us tons of expensive gifts. Instead, she took the time and energy to prepare a magical day for us that we enjoyed so much. It didn't matter what the gift was by the end of it, because we had had so much fun on the journey.

I don't remember how we celebrated Christmas the year that Vincent disappeared, I'm not sure that we did. I just know that the following year I did my best to make a treasure hunt for mum, leaving envelopes out just like she (Santa) did. I think that meant a lot to her. I'd saved up my pocket money to buy her a picture frame and put a photo of the three of us in. She kept it on her bedside table for a while, but I think it made her sad. One day, it had been removed and replaced by another picture. We never spoke about it.

That first Christmas after The War started was one of the hardest. The snow made the outside world look almost normal, but if you looked hard enough, you could still see the devastation. I remember wondering whether the snow would be enough to wipe out the Dead for good, and maybe it would be the start of civilisation rebuilding itself. Surely the snow would cause the Dead to freeze.

By this point, I wasn't seeing a daily horde of the Dead walking past my window, so I couldn't see any of the frozen ones up close. I could use the telescope to view the ones in the city centre, but it was difficult to tell if they were frozen dead, or just dead dead. They weren't moving, but it didn't mean their brains were out of commission. Until the brain is destroyed, they can survive anything. I kept waiting for a group of the living to come by and kill them all in their frozen state, but it never happened. I should have gone out there myself, but the city centre felt too far away. Besides, after what happened the last time I went out there, I had decided that I wasn't going to leave the house until all this was over. I had stopped taking care of myself at this point. I never really showered or washed my hair. I figured that there was no one around, therefore no need to look after my personal hygiene anymore. My hair had grown extremely long, greasy and matted, as there was no one to cut it for me. It was pretty gross.

Ever wondered what makes your head snow,
When your hair starts to grow?
Dan Druff is this pesky creature's name,
Decorating your shoulders is his evil game.
All the shampoo in the world won't get rid of him,
It will just temporarily keep a lid on him.

Then just as he's out of sight and you think you've won the fight,
He'll be sure to ruin your night by painting your shoulders white.

He's made of strong stuff, that little Dan Druff.

Frank asked me about the snow back then. He asked me if he would be getting presents for Christmas because it was snowing. I had no idea how he knew about Christmas or even what snow was. I still don't understand where he gets these random pieces of information from. I know for a fact that I hadn't spoken to him about any of those things, and there's no way he could have seen snow before. As usual, when I asked him how he knew this information, he looked at me like I'd asked him to decode the foreign language I had just spoken to him in. I asked him to tell me where he thought the snow had come from. He told me some bizarre story about how there were two clouds that lived above our house; a mummy cloud and a daddy cloud. They were always fighting, and you could tell which cloud was winning the fight because if the mummy cloud was winning, it would be sunny, and if the daddy cloud was winning, it would be rainy. I shrugged it off as the ramblings of a demented cretin, and asked him that if that were the case, where did the snow come from? He explained that at Christmas time, they stopped fighting for a while and when they weren't fighting, it would be snowy.

After hearing Frank's mad explanation for why it was snowing outside, I felt overcome with a feeling of pity. I felt sorry for him for some reason. I don't really know why. I decided I would try and do something for him, so I searched the house for something I could give to him as a Christmas present. To be honest, I could have just wrapped up a rock from the garden and he probably would have been quite happy, so there really was no need to go to such efforts, but I did. I found mum's travel bag in the garage and inside was an eye mask that she used on long journeys. I selfishly thought that this might help to get Frank to sleep at night, or at the very least it might help him with the night terrors. I wrapped it up using some old paper I found in the office. The whole process took a lot longer than it should have, with most of the time spent trying to find the end piece of the sellotape to wrap the gift. Cack hands.

Once it was finally ready, I took the gift downstairs to where Frank was patiently waiting and handed it to him. Before he unwrapped it, he got all excited and told me to wait. He tottered off and came back a minute or so later, clutching an envelope in his little useless sausage arms. He handed it to me and said merry Christmas. I opened the envelope to find a card inside with a poorly drawn Christmas tree on the front, and what I can only assume were supposed to be drawings of me and Frank standing in front of it holding hands. Inside the card, Frank had crudely written in crayon:

Hapee Crismas Edwood

Pleese dont be sad aneemore

Lots off love

Yur best frend fraNk

I remember feeling quite touched at the gesture. I had no idea that he had prepared anything for me. I also had no idea what day of the year it really was, but that didn't matter, we treated that day like it was Christmas day. We made a feast out of some of the nicer food I had been saving and we went into the back garden to build snowmen. This was back in the days before the dead garden gnome began roaming around out there. We even lit the fireplace in the Den and made hot chocolate using the nasty tasting long life milk. All things considered, it was a pretty perfect day.

That night, after he'd opened his gift, I tried to explain to Frank how to use his eye mask. It took an in depth 45-minute explanation, but by the end of it he said he understood and went off to bed all by himself. Soon after, I went up to check on him and saw that he hadn't attached the eye mask to his face like I had explained. Instead, he was holding on to it while he slept, like a baby holding onto a comforter. He still sleeps with it to this day.

The festive cheer eventually came to an end when the Dead began to thaw. The days spent observing them through the telescope hoping that this was the beginning of the end were wasted. The Dead had unfrozen and were walking once again.

It's been at least a year and it's snowing once again today. This time however, there is barely any food left in the pantry, other than the vegetables I've managed to harvest. I really hope the snow doesn't destroy what else we've got growing in the garden. I need to think about how to cover up and protect the vegetable patches without getting bitten by that evil garden gnome. More importantly, I think I need to sort out what I'm getting Frank for Christmas this year.

Extras

I've mentioned that my mum used to keep cages of creatures in her room for her experiments and things. It wasn't anything horrible. She wasn't spraying perfume in their eyes or anything like that. She was never cruel to them. I know that she took good care of them and gave them names and would be upset if they passed away. Different creatures would come and go, sometimes the cages would all be full and sometimes only one or two of them would be occupied. The ones that stick out in my mind were the orange and black striped cat that looked like a little tiger and could break glass with its voice, the tiny pocket sized orangutan who used sign language to share sonnets, the strange goblin boy who smelled so bad that he had to live in a smell proof bubble to protect the rest of the household, a cute miniature elephant that could play music through his trunk, my pet chameleon spent a fair amount of time in there despite supposedly belonging to me, and of course Spike, the emo vampire bat with no teeth.

Although these creatures would come and go, there was always one constant throughout; a little Spanish mouse called Squib. He was the most interesting of all the creatures and I believe he was mum's favourite. If he wasn't in his cage at home, then he would be in his carry case on the way to the lab with her. Squib's cage was the biggest one in the room which might seem odd considering he was a very small mouse, but it was due to Squib's special ability that he needed to have such a large space to live in. I only ever saw it happen once, but when the mouse felt a strong emotion, such as fear or anger, he would triple in size and turn into a ferocious beast, almost like a werewolf. Like so many of my memories, I was quite young at the time but I remember waking up in the middle of the night after hearing a loud crashing noise coming from mum's room, running to her bedroom and forcing open the door without knocking to see this horrible blood-curdling monstrosity with glowing red eyes in the corner of the room, and my mum holding up her desk chair as a shield while she tried to calm it down. When I cried out, my mum simply replied, "it's OK, it's just Squib. Go back bed." She was so calm in her delivery, almost as if I were foolish for being worried in the first place. The next day she told me that Squib would never hurt her, he just got scared when she tried to take a blood sample from him, and he reacted in a normal way as he felt threatened. She told me to finish my bowl of cereal

and to stop worrying. I noticed that she didn't say anything about Squib never hurting me. I avoided going into mum's room much after that.

Squib had an interesting way of communicating with people. He couldn't speak or sign, but he could squeak in such a way that mum and her colleagues could understand what he was saying. He had a form of super intelligence and communication skills which made him an invaluable resource to mum's research, but there was always the unpredictable risk that he was going to explode at any moment, like a stick of dynamite.

The last time I saw Squib was the night mum left. He was never in focus when I was speaking to her for the last time, but he was definitely somewhere in the background. All the cages had been emptied, Squib's was the only one I remember seeing occupied. When I think back to that last conversation I had with mum, I don't recall her giving me any instructions regarding Squib. Unsurprisingly, I had bigger things on my mind at the time, so feeding that little mouse monster wasn't on my list of fish to fry. I can only assume that her lack of instruction regarding the mouse meant that she intended to take him with her. I don't recall seeing her holding his carry case when she left, although it was difficult to notice anything through the tears in my eyes.

It wasn't until I went to close mum's bedroom door the day after she had left that I thought about Squib. I walked into the room and noticed that his cage was empty, and the door was open. Did she take him with her? Did she forget about him? Had he escaped? Then I saw the coffee cup she had left out for Spike, and I forgot all about the mouse. I'm ashamed to admit that I had completely forgotten all about Squib. That is, until yesterday.

I was in the garden for most of the morning, attempting to fend off the dead garden gnome while picking carrots. In the end, I just put a big bucket over him. He was making a hell of a lot of noise under there which wasn't ideal, but it meant I could tend to the garden without worrying about the safety of my biteable ankles. Just as my harvesting session was coming to an end, I felt a sharp pain in my hand like someone had jabbed me with a needle. I looked at my hand but couldn't see anything. As I pulled the last carrot out of the earth I felt it again, this time the pain was even sharper, like a bite. I had a worrying thought that somehow the gnome must have tunneled under the bucket and all the way to the carrot patch and bitten me when the last carrot was lifted. I glanced back, but the bucket with legs behind me put that theory to bed. I inspected my hand again and noticed two little red dots which looked remarkably similar to insect bites. Had I been bitten by two bugs at the exact same time? I was suddenly reminded of the time Frank had tried to iron the creases out of his arms, and I was left with third degree burns. I looked around for him and remembered that ever since the dead garden gnome had appeared,

Frank refused to come out here. This could only mean one thing; Frank was somewhere inside the house 'entertaining' himself. This could be very dangerous.

After a short walk around the house and another sharp pain in my hand, I discovered Frank sprawled out on the floor of the garage, his face pressed to the floor and his arm shoved into what looked like a mouse hole in the skirting board.

INT. The garage. Morning.
Edward approaches Frank who is trying to reach further into the mouse hole. Frank turns his head to face the very confused looking Edward.

Edward: Frank! What are you doing?
Frank: Looking for my friend.
Edward: Who?
Frank: I don't know his name, but he likes to bite.
Edward: If he's biting you, why are you looking for him?
Frank: Because he's hungry.

Edward rolls his eyes in a way that expresses his disinterest in the conversation and then picks Frank up off the ground.

This wasn't the first time that Frank had located some strange creature running around the house, but it was the first time that he had been bitten. Given the fact that we currently live in a world where getting bitten can be quite detrimental to your existence, this was quite alarming.

I had no idea what I was going to find inside that hole in the wall, but I knew I had to investigate. What if it was another garden gnome situation? Was there going to be some other decorative garden ornament that had come to life in there? I wouldn't be able to leave without knowing. Also, if it was something that had been reanimated, it had just bitten Frank and technically bitten me, so I needed to know if we were going to turn.

I bent down and brought my eyes level with the hole in the skirting board only to be greeted by nothing but pitch-black darkness. Just as I was about to get back up, the hole was suddenly filled with one large red glowing eye, and I heard a snarling sound echo around every wall of the cold garage. It was Squib. Not the cute little mouse version, but the horrible beastie version. Frank must have done something to upset him to bring on this state of mutation. I decided not to question Frank on his theories about why this may have occurred as I knew it would be a long time before that conversation resulted in anything close to helpful. Instead, I slowly backed away and ushered Frank towards the door that led back into the house. I quietly closed the door behind us and gently moved a large chest of drawers in front of the entrance to the garage just in case the mouse monster decided to follow us.

This morning, I returned to the garage armed with a weapon. I didn't know what to expect so I thought I would prepare for the worst. The garage was empty, no sign of any giant mice in any of the corners. I approached the hole in the wall and called out the mouse's name.

"Squib?"

I was greeted by a very soft squeak which sounded remarkably like "sí."

The tiny little mouse crawled out from his hole. He looked so much smaller than I remembered. I don't mean smaller compared to his monstrous alter ego, I mean he looked like he'd been starved half to death. "Are you hungry?" I asked. "Sí" replied Squib.

The little mouse followed me back into the house and through to the pantry where we still had some very old and very smelly cheese. Before I could apologise for the lack of cheddar-based options, the mouse jumped into the centre of the wheel of cheese as if it were a paddling pool and was doing his very best to eat his way to the deep end.

Once the little mouse had eaten himself into a cheese coma, he looked a lot more like I remembered him. A little plump white mouse with a pink tail and huge ears. I spent the next few hours trying to communicate with him. Unfortunately, I am not proficient in the language of mice, even though Squib's squeaks are clearly trying to convey meaning, I struggle with anything more than yes/no answers. The following are some of the questions and answers we covered:

I. Have you been here this whole time? **No**
II. Where have you been? **Indecipherable**
III. How long have you been in the garage? **Three squeaks**
IV. Do you know what happened to mum? **Sí**

It was unclear if his three squeaks meant three days, weeks, or months but I thought it was interesting that he hadn't been here this whole time. Where had he been? It's questions like this that make me wish I had paid more attention in Spanish class. However, all this information paled in comparison with the mouse's knowledge of what had happened to mum. When I pressed him for more information on the subject he started to run out of the room. He paused at the door and looked back at me in a way that told me I needed to follow him. He ran through the hallway and around the corner towards the front door. When I caught up with him, he was stood up on his back legs, his tiny paw touching the front door. I think he wanted me to go outside so he could lead me to her. I didn't know what to do. I still don't. There is a chance that this little mouse knows where she is, but there is also a much stronger chance that he doesn't, and that he would just run away as soon as the front door is opened. I did what I could to explain to him why we couldn't go out there. It looked very much like he shook his head in shame before walking back towards the garage. There is a chance I am reading too much into that though. The front door remains boarded up to this day and for good reason. I opened it up once earlier this year and it didn't go well. I can't go back out there. I just can't.

I went back into the garage this afternoon but didn't hear any squeaks and couldn't see anything in the mouse hole. I even let Frank put his arm in the hole, but nothing happened. I don't know if Squib is still running around the house somewhere or if he's gone for good this time. I do wish I could be brave. I wish that I could tear off the boards on the front door and follow Squib wherever it was he was trying to take me. I just can't though. Too much has happened, and I can't take the risk.

Frank has been inconsolable for the last few hours. When I asked him what was wrong, he told me that he misses his friend. It never occurred to me that he might be lonely. He has never experienced any other way of living and isolation is all he has ever known. To suddenly have something or someone new introduced to him only for it to be immediately taken away is understandably upsetting.

Frank isn't speaking to me right now. I don't blame him. I wouldn't be speaking to me either.

Treading The Boards

It took a tremendously long time to board up every door and window in the house. The hardest part was finding enough wood for the job. Once we had used all the materials in the shed and brought in the shed itself, we had to start breaking down furniture and parts of the house - the banister from the staircase, cupboard doors, anything else we could get our hands on. At one point, in our search for wooden objects, Frank brought me the guitar (the one that he isn't allowed to touch and shouldn't have even known where to find due to its secret hiding place). Luckily, we didn't have to resort to using it. I reckon it took us around three weeks to finish destroying things and nailing them to the doors and windows.

I remember on one of the last days of boarding up all the windows, Frank and I were on the second floor, and I was hammering the nails as softly as I could to avoid making too much noise. Frank was stood behind me, performing the extremely important task of holding onto the next nail that I'd need to use. We hadn't boarded up mum's room yet – I was putting this off for as long as possible. I asked Frank for the second time to hand me another nail. He often had to be reminded of his simple but apparently complex duty. After my third request went unheard, I noticed that he was staring at something.

"What's that?" he asked, pointing at one of the wooden boards we had just nailed to the wall. There was a name faintly carved into one of the boards which read:

Vincent

Underneath, there was some barely legible faded text written in crayon that read:

Please come home

Growing up, Vincent and I used to play outside in what we called the playhouse. It was basically a shed with a window and a lockable door, with the lock on the outside. We would spend hours playing in there, pretending it was something else like a castle or a laboratory. I remember one time, Vincent locked me in the shed and pretended to disappear. I called out for him in a panic and then he opened the door to console me. It's horrible to think that only a few short years later he would disappear for real.

The first time I returned to the playhouse/garden shed after Vincent disappeared was the day after mum chose to stop searching for him. Although she hadn't been well due to the grief of missing him and the stress of the search, I think it was the search that kept her going. The day after I asked her to stop searching, the reality really hit her hard. Although the search had finally come to an end at my own request, the grieving process had only just begun. Whatever I said, whatever I did, I couldn't get mum to get out of bed. It was like she was in a trance.

Soon after, it was Mother's Day, which was obviously a very tough day. I made her a card and left it in a pink envelope on her bedside table. I know now that she was depressed, but at the time I didn't really understand what that meant. I remember thinking that the only thing that would make her happy again would be to see Vincent. A foolish part of me thought there was a chance that he was hiding in the shed. Why I hadn't thought of that months ago when everyone was searching, I don't know. Surely someone must have checked the shed. Right?

I left mum and ran outside full of naive hope to check the contents of the shed. It will come as no surprise to anyone reading this that my older brother had not been sitting in the shed, patiently waiting for someone to find him for the past few months. I burst into the shed out of breath only to be greeted by... nothing at all. What happened to me next has always bothered me because I don't know if it was a dream or reality. There is a chance that I ran into the shed so fast that I hit my head and blacked out, and so the following could have been some sort of concussion dream. But there is also the possibility that, somehow, it was all real. After all, I do live in a world where the Dead walk the Earth, and a living voodoo doll shares my DNA...

As I was stood in the middle of the hollow garden shed with the door slamming shut behind me, I heard the sharp sound of the deadbolt locking into place. I turned my head to look through the tiny shed window, which seemed to be letting in much less light than it had just a moment ago. I couldn't see any sign of a person out there. Who had locked the door? I tried to open the door, but as hard as I tried, I couldn't open it. I called out for my mum but was greeted by a chilly silence. Another glance through the solitary window revealed the silhouette of the scarecrow in the garden. Had he been there a minute ago?

I spent the next few minutes banging on the shed door; the only way in or out. Despite still being inside the property boundary, I felt very scared. The light streaming through the window dimmed again to almost nothing, as if the movie projector bulb had blown from overuse. I was filled with an overwhelming sense of dread like something terrible was about to happen, but

I didn't know what. I looked to the left of me, and it felt like the world was slowing down to one frame per second, but then I turned to the right, and it was as if the world was suddenly on fast forward. The light disappeared entirely, but it felt like there were people all around me, looking at me.

My third glance at the window revealed the scarecrow had somehow moved closer to the shed. Despite the pitch-black darkness that surrounded the shot, the pumpkin headed scarecrow was now perfectly lit. I took a step backwards, tripped over something that wasn't there, and began falling into a bottomless pit of darkness for what seemed like hours. I don't understand why my memories of this event are so vivid. Nothing else from that period of my life stands out like this.

I finally stopped falling, and the bottom of the bottomless pit turned out to be nothing more than the wooden floor of the shed. Why had it felt like I was falling for so long? Questions like this led me to believe it was all a dream, but that doesn't explain the writing on the wall...

As I lay on the shed floor in total darkness, I saw a lightning strike illuminate the window, revealing the carved face of the pumpkin, backlit to perfection by what looked like a golden hour sunset. Another crackle of lightning revealed a name carved into the wall of the shed. **Vincent**. How did this get there? How long had it been there for? I have no memory of him carving this and no memory of ever seeing it before. Had he come back? A third lightning strike came crashing down onto the roof of the shed. A key light aimed directly at the scarecrow showed that it was now standing inside the shed, staring down at me. The sound of thunder followed, but the light didn't fade away this time. The carved eyes of the rotten fruit narrowed as its gaze intensified. I heard a voice in my head. It was Vincent's voice. My brother… He began a monologue that I will never forget:

Edward. Breathe. Breathe. Everything is going to be OK. It will pass. You are going to be alright. You can take this moment to mourn, you are allowed to be sad, and you are permitted to weep. But once this moment is over, I am going to need you to be strong. You will need to take care of mum. She is going to need you now more than ever. Take care of yourself so that you can take better care of her. Do this for me brother. I know that you are able. You need to be brave. Breathe. Breathe.

I woke up.

It was morning.

I was laying on the floor of the shed, bathed in sunlight. There was no sign of the scarecrow, no damage from the lightning, no voices or sounds to be heard, except the singing of the birds in the trees outside. I sat up and looked around the tiny space that had once felt so giant, trying to reassemble the fragile puzzle pieces of my memory now scattered around my mind. I had no idea what was real anymore. Not until I saw the carving in the wall. It was still there, and it looked exactly as it had in my dream, or whatever it was that I experienced the night before. It was right there in front of me. I could run my fingers across the letters that looked like they had been clawed into the wood.

Vincent

I didn't know what to think. I didn't know what to believe.

I slumped down to the floor and saw something in between the wooden floorboards of the shed; a small red crayon. Without thinking or planning, I picked up the crayon and began writing on the wall beneath the carving.

Please come home

The puzzle pieces in my mind fell into place to form the full picture of what had happened the night before. I stood up and ran out of the shed, past the creepy scarecrow who was now back in his usual position in the garden, protecting the crops from unwanted visitors, and ran back to the house with the absolute intention of sharing the image in my head with mum so that she could see and feel what I could. The strange feeling of anxious excitement that had been bubbling inside me disappeared almost immediately as I stepped inside the house. Something equally as strange as what I'd experienced the night before, appeared to have also occurred inside the house.

When I left the house yesterday, all the walls were decorated in bright, vibrant colours. Today, the walls appeared very different indeed. Every wall in every room of the house was painted black. How long had I been gone for? There was no way that mum could have painted the entire house in one night. This would have taken a team of decorators all night to accomplish. I touched one of the walls expecting to feel wet paint on my fingers, but the wall was bone dry. The walls weren't freshly painted at all – they were transformed. It was as if the house had picked up on mum's emotions and had reflected her feelings on the walls, like some kind of mood ring. I walked up the stairs in amazement as I saw that all the walls upstairs had also been subject to this gothic makeover.

As I approached mum's bedroom door, I remembered what Vincent's voice had told me about being strong and looking after her. I opened the bedroom door and saw her face and decided right then and there that I wouldn't tell her about what had happened the night before, or at least what I thought had happened. I wouldn't tell her about the carving in the shed wall or about the voice in my head and what it told me. This decision was very easy to make when I saw that mum was sat up in bed holding her Mother's Day card, with a huge smile on her face. It was the first time I had seen her smile in months. I couldn't do it to her, I couldn't give her any more false hope. She needed to grieve in her own way just as I had to grieve in mine. I won't say that everything was OK after that moment, because it wasn't. Mum was sad for a long time, and so was I. We helped each other get better though. Each passing day was a little bit easier.

I spent a large portion of my day telling this story to Frank instead of boarding up the windows like I'd planned. He stared blankly at me for the most part, but he did ask a few choice questions such as "Why was Vincent a scary pumpkin man?", and "Why haven't the walls changed colour again?", to which I am sad to say I had no answers for.

I had a look at the carving in the wooden board today and was reminded of how sad it was to tear down our childhood playhouse. Vincent never did come back. I never heard his voice again. I have experienced a lot of strange and unexplainable things in my life, but that night in the shed, hearing my brother's voice in my head, is the one I have always wanted to be explained the most.

ACT IV

Act IV - The Villain

Every story needs a villain, and this is my reckoning of the time I met one.

For the longest time, I would have proclaimed that the Dead were the villains of this tale, or at least whoever is responsible for creating them. There are a lot of strange creatures under this roof and even one on top of it, but none of them are bad guys, not even the vampire in the basement. Growing up, my brother told me stories of some pretty nasty creatures that could be considered villains. The worst one to my mind is The Gleeken. I don't think a day goes by that I don't think about it.

In the dead of the night when your dreams start to deepen,
You drift off to sleep and your jaw starts to weaken,
Your mouth begins to open, and it acts like a beacon,
To the depraved little creature that is named The Gleeken.

As you start to snore and your mouth opens wider,
This nasty thing crawls on your bed like a giant spider.
The vile little monster has only one sinister idea,
And that's to fill your mouth with its filthy diarrhoea.

When morning comes and your breath smells like poo,
You'll know The Gleeken has been and gone number two.
You can clean your teeth before bed as much as you like,
It just provides a cleaner surface for The Gleeken to strike,
No matter what you do, don't fall asleep, don't even take a nap,
Because The Gleeken will come, and he'll take a big crap.

The idea of The Gleeken was spawned in my brother's head one day when I asked him why my breath always smelled so bad in the mornings. I don't think he realised that his little story about a nightmarish creature who defecates in your mouth while you are sleeping would have such a traumatic effect on me. My brother wasn't a villain for telling me stories that scared me, he was a hero because he was there for me when I couldn't sleep and for reading me stories regardless of how late it was. I think that him telling me stories was his way of connecting with me.

The villain of the piece is someone who is solely responsible for all the harm and trouble that takes place during the scene. This next scene takes place earlier this year, before I started writing in this diary and before Death started hanging around outside the house, like some kind of creepy skeletal stalker. It was scenes like this that made me feel like I needed to start writing things down.

The scene opens with a wide establishing shot of the street, the camera pans left to slowly reveal the large gothic mansion that is my house. We crane down to the third-floor window where a figure can be seen. As the shot pulls forward, I am revealed to be standing at the circular window next to the telescope. We jump cut to the house interior and see a mid-shot of me looking through the viewfinder, with Frank stood by my feet, chewing on a coffee table coaster that he has mistaken for a pancake. The silent room tone is suddenly interrupted by the sound of shouting off in the distance. I quickly move the telescope's direction and the scene transitions to a point of view shot. The audience now sees through the view finder to the street below. The shot shifts from left to right until its subjects are located. Two men are seen running down the street towards the house, one man is chasing the other. As they move closer to the foreground of the shot, it becomes clear that the larger man is giving chase and the smaller one is quite young, and seems to be getting younger and younger the closer he gets to the camera.

The larger of the two men is dressed all in black, has no hair and wears an eye patch over his left eye. He appears to be old and looks tired, his face covered in scars and wrinkles. His hands are stained with blood and his shoes are old and worn out. He might be the most unfriendly person I have ever seen and is certainly not someone you would want chasing you.

The second of the two does not look much older than me. He is wearing a red tracksuit and a matching backpack with what looks like the end of a baseball bat sticking out of the top of it. His brown hair is long and scruffy, and his facial hair is clearly still in the research and development stage. His young eyes are filled with genuine terror as he looks behind him to see that the older man is closing the distance between them.

No more than ten metres away from the burnt-out car outside the house, the older man tackled the young boy to the ground and started trying to place his hands around the boy's throat. A new sound effect is added to the track out of nowhere; the sound of the Dead – two of them, walking towards the car from the opposite direction. They must have been close by and alerted by the noise.

I didn't understand. The War was supposed to be between the living and the Dead. Why was this horrible old man trying to hurt this boy? Why, when there is an army of reanimated corpses wandering around, would someone try to attack a living human being? These questions were racing through my head unanswered when I realised that I was running down the stairs. I hadn't instructed my body to do this and yet, there it went. In a matter of moments, I was stood in front of the boarded up front door. What was I doing? Was I about to go outside for the first time since my failed mission to rescue Victoria, in a pathetic attempt to save this random boy from not only the Dead, but also the living? Once again, without receiving any direction from my brain, my body was moving. My hands were desperately trying to pull the wooden boards down from the door. Once my brain caught up with my body it decided that this job would require more than just my hands. As if by magic, I found a hammer lying on the ground, almost exactly where I needed one to be. As I started pulling out nails from the boards with the back of the hammer, I noticed something out of the corner of my eye that hadn't been there a moment ago.

INT. Hallway. Afternoon.
Edward is doing his best to tear down the boards that are blocking the front door to the house, protecting him from the world outside. Spike enters stage left in his vampire form.

Spike: Edward! What the hell are you doing?
Edward: There's someone out there who needs my help.
Spike: You know you can't go out there, you'll die. I won't protect you.
Edward: I don't need you to protect me, but I do need you to help me get these boards off.

A cry of "Help" can be heard from the other side of the door.

Spike: Leave them to die. Don't go out there Edward.

Edward ignores the vampire's advice and continues to rip the nails from the boards. He cuts his hand removing a loose nail and blood starts to drip from the wound.

Edward: Help me get these boards off!

Spike looks at the blood with a ravenous look in his eyes. He closes them and puts both of his hands on his head.

Spike: No.

With his eyes still closed and his hands on his head, Spike turns and walks towards the basement. Edward ignores the cut on his hand and continues bringing down the boards. A sharp pain in Edward's shoulder tells him that Frank must be clumsily making his way down the stairs. When only a few boards remain, Frank appears at the top of the first-floor staircase, looking down.

Frank: What's happening?
Edward: Nothing Frank, don't worry. Go back upstairs.
Frank: Are we going outside today?
Edward: No, we're not… we're going to… we're going to play hide and seek.
Frank: Yay! I go first?
Edward: Yes, you go and hide somewhere upstairs, and I'll come and look for you.
Frank: OK! Count to six.

Frank waddles off in hurried excitement as Edward pulls off the final board. Edward opens the door.

When I got outside, the old man had the boy pinned down, his hands around his throat. Without thinking about the consequences, I shouted "Stop" as loud as I could, completely forgetting about the dead people fast approaching from the other direction. The walking dead bodies had their sights fixed on the two living men in front of them, so the sound of my voice had no impact on their course of action. However, my shout had distracted the old man enough to enable the boy to land a punch on the side of his head, which proved enough to allow him to wrestle himself free just before the dead men entered the tableau. The dead men simultaneously fell on top of the stunned old man, and he quickly joined them in death as the boy looked on.

I shouted to the boy "Over here". At first the boy looked confused, like he was trying to figure out if this was some sort of trick. I signaled for him to come over with one hand, keeping the other firmly on the front door. The boy looked back at the bloody remains of the old man. He quickly weighed up his options and began running towards me.

A part of me was scared. I didn't know what to do or even what to say when he got here. I hadn't spoken to anyone other than a dimwitted voodoo doll, a foul-mouthed gargoyle and a moody vampire for months, maybe years. What the hell was I going to say to this kid, who up close, now looked much older than me. The Dead looked like they were almost finished with their lunch, so I skipped the pleasantries and simply told the boy to get inside.

As soon as we were both inside, I closed the door and immediately began hammering the boards back up. Without saying a word to each other, the stranger picked up a board and started to help. As soon as we were done, I signaled for him to stay where he was, while I checked on the situation outside through the third-floor window. On my way up the stairs, I spotted Frank's legs sticking out from under my bed, hiding like a good voodoo doll. He would be safe there for a few hours at least. Looking out of the third-floor window, I didn't need the telescope to see the two dead men wandering away down the street, off to enjoy the rest of their unlives. I returned downstairs, softly closing my bedroom door as I went by.

The stranger was standing where I left him. As soon as he saw me, he enquired if they were gone. I told him that we were safe. The stranger began rummaging in his red backpack for something. He produced a small roll of bandages and handed them to me. "For your hand" he said, referring to the cut I'd received from prying the boards off the front door. I thanked him and told him not to worry as I had a first aid box that hadn't seen much action. I didn't want to tell him that it was usually used for wrapping up burns on my limbs from when Frank had fallen asleep pressed up against the radiator. This guy looked like he had seen some real action and probably suffered some real injuries. Plus, telling him about Frank before I had even introduced myself would probably have just freaked him out, and wasn't something I wanted to do.

I introduced myself and he did the same. He told me his name was Artemis, but that I could call him Art, which I thought was the coolest name I'd ever heard. He told me about his experience of The War since it had started and how he had been part of a group of other survivors up until recently. As much as he knew about the outside world, he still couldn't tell me how this all started, he knew as little as I did on that subject. He didn't seem to be overly concerned about it though. I couldn't believe how calm he was about the whole situation in general. He thanked me for saving his life like you would thank someone for holding the door open for you. As he was talking, I noticed that his tracksuit wasn't red at all; it was actually white, but it was almost completely covered in blood. He explained that before the old man tried to kill him, he had taken down a 'Geek' and got covered in its blood. He said the group he was with referred to the Dead as Geeks. Art said he always knew that one day Geeks would rule the world, he just didn't realise it would look like this.

Art took off his tracksuit jacket to reveal a black T-shirt with NOT DEAD YET crudely written in white lettering. I decided not to question this. I offered to put his tracksuit in the washing machine but warned him there was a strong chance that it would come out smelling of sick, but at least it would be clean. He thanked me and asked if I had any food. At first, I thought it was because he was hungry, but realised he was asking for my sake. He produced a packet of sweets from his bag, the type you would get when you went to the cinema. He said they were the last of his supplies, but he would gladly share them with me as gratitude for my hospitality. I couldn't believe it. Those sweets were all he had left, and he was willing to share them with me. I thanked him and explained that I had plenty of food and that he was welcome to have some.

I have never seen such a look of pure amazement on someone's face as I did when Art saw the pantry for the first time. Before he saw the food supply, he was commenting on how he didn't understand how I had lasted so long on my own. He asked me how I found this house, and I explained that it was mine and that I had been here since the start. Art said that he had been bouncing around different places almost every week since the start, never staying in one place for too long. When I asked him why that was, he explained that it wasn't just the Dead that you had to fear out there, it was the living as well. I told him that today was the first time I'd seen a living person attack another human being. He smiled and shook his head sadly. He told me that this is the reality out there now… "The world is dead, we're just living in it."

We had something to eat and spoke about our lives before The War. It turned out that we had a lot in common. We both shared a love of the cinema, and he mentioned that he'd spent some time living in an abandoned cinema not too long ago. Our favourite band was The Pink Bunnies, we both played guitar and even shared the same level of disinterest in sports and other outdoor activities. Unsurprisingly, our biggest common theme was that we had both lost people in The War. Art told me that he had lost his entire family early on, and how he had been travelling by himself. He said that every time he started running with a new group, eventually he would be the last man standing. I couldn't really relate considering I had only ventured outside of my front door once since this all started, and that resulted in Victoria getting killed. I decided not to tell Art about that. Even though I felt comfortable with him and like I'd known him for years, I didn't want him to know about Victoria. I still felt ashamed and wasn't ready to relive that memory yet.

It had been several hours since Art's arrival, and Frank still hadn't emerged from his secret hiding place. While Art and I talked, I thought about how to best explain Frank, the living voodoo doll who shares my DNA. The perfect segue failed to present itself, but when Art asked if I had anything to drink, I thought I could ease him into the weirdness of the house by introducing him to the bar gnome first. After all, a magical talking garden gnome that prepares cocktails is much less disturbing than a talking voodoo doll with no eyelids. Right?

We walked into the dining room, and I announced that I was going to show him a magic trick. He understandably looked perplexed. I announced my drink order to the world in general expecting to hear the usual clinking of bottles coming from inside the bar. The diegetic sound of the scene was pure silence. I opened the bar to investigate what was taking so long, and was greeted with a handwritten note that read:

ERROR
The service you require is currently unavailable. Please try again later.
GONE ON BREAK. MAKE YOUR OWN DAMN DRINK!

I was baffled, but not nearly as much as Art must have been. I'd never seen the bar gnome leave the safety of his drinks cabinet. This was really strange. I mean, not as strange as the existence of the tiny clay figurine that lives inside the bar, but still pretty odd. I apologised to Art for the bogus announcement of a magic trick and made him a drink by hand. Judging by his tolerance of alcohol, I estimated that he was a few years older than me at least, and had likely had quite a few alcoholic beverages in his time. He told me he was sixteen when The War started, which meant he must've been about eighteen years old now.

We took our drinks into the Den and sat by the fireplace. I decided not to tell him about my magical little pet chameleon that sometimes lives in the chimney and keeps the fire burning just in case that he had disappeared too. The longer Art was in the house, the more difficult I found it to broach the subject of all the strange creatures who roam this property. We discussed my video game collection instead. It's a bizarre thing to admit but there were times when I was speaking to Art that I completely forgot about the world outside and all the chaos out there. This was the first conversation that I'd had with a human being in such a long time.

Art asked me how many Geeks I had killed. Without going into too much detail about the purpose of my mission on the day Victoria died, I told Art about my encounter with Mrs. Jones and her watermelon skull. Art explained that the reason her head had burst open so easily was due to her age. He told me a story about how he and his brother had recently taken down a bunch of older Geeks and that their skulls were incredibly easy to destroy. As engrossed as I was in his story, I couldn't help but notice a contradiction in the narrative. Earlier, he mentioned that his whole family had all been killed, and that he had been travelling alone for a while with no mention of his brother. I thought it was a little odd, but decided not to bring it up in case it was a sensitive subject.

At some point in the evening, Art asked if he could use the bathroom. I racked my brain thinking about whether there were any terrifying creatures he might bump into in there, but decided that he should be fine as long as he didn't use the hot tap. There was always the chance he might meet someone or something on the journey there and back, but the bathroom is usually unoccupied most of the time. Art disappeared for quite a while, which made me worry that he had gotten lost on his way back. I stood up to go and find him, and noticed that Art had left his backpack with me in the Den. Something about the bag struck me as odd but I couldn't work out what it was. On closer inspection, I clocked the baseball bat sticking out of the open zipper. It looked remarkably like mine. The same one I had left outside Victoria's house on that horrible day. There was no way it was the same bat, but I couldn't help checking it out. I slowly pulled the bat out of the bag and noticed that it had the same markings as mine - three small chrome claw marks left over from the fight with the Dead outside Victoria's house. I was so deeply entranced by the bat that I didn't even notice that Art had re-entered the room.

Art didn't seem angry that I'd gone through his bag, but he did ask me what I was doing. I tried to explain that I thought it could be my black steel baseball bat that I lost all that time ago. I realised how petty it must have sounded to him. Here's me with this big house, a pantry full of food, with a drink in my hand and a fireplace in the background; and there was Art with almost nothing in the world other than the possessions in his backpack. He had already offered me his bandages and what remained of his food supply, now it looked like I was trying to steal his only weapon. The scene must have looked awful to him.

He told me that he had found the bat around the corner from my house, which made perfect sense. The only problem was that he said he had found it somewhere between here and the city centre. Apparently, he was on a supply run in the city when he came across the bat. This didn't make sense because Victoria's house was in the opposite direction to the city centre. Why was he lying?

After our discussion about the bat's rightful ownership, Art told me he would gladly return it to me. He'd clearly been through a lot recently, so I chose not to press him for more information on how he'd found the bat in a completely different location to where I had left it. There were lots of plausible reasons for how he could've found the bat. I didn't need to probe him for more details, and I didn't want to either. I also didn't want to ask him why it had taken him so long to go to the bathroom, as that could have been quite awkward.

We continued talking long into the night. It might sound foolish of me, but I felt that we were establishing a connection and I felt like we were becoming friends. Art had so much knowledge, he was full of interesting facts, such as 'up to a third of the weight of your pillow is made up of dead skin, bugs, and their faeces'. Like I needed another reason to stop me sleeping at night. He had a pretty dark sense of humour, but I guess you have to find some way of coping at the end of the world. The more time I spent with Art, the more I wanted to know about him. I couldn't help but wonder if he felt the same about me. He asked me how I'd managed to survive all this time on my own and told me that if he'd been locked up in here for the same length of time, it would have probably driven him crazy.

Art asked me if it was OK for him to stay overnight and set out again in the morning. It upset me that he wanted to leave. I kind of assumed that he'd want to stay here. But I told him it was fine and that he could stay as long as he wanted. Without giving it much thought, I offered him Vincent's old bedroom as Frank was still playing hide and seek like a pro and was unlikely to be sleeping in there tonight. It was only when I showed Art to the bedroom that it hit me. The reason I enjoyed having him in the house with me was because he reminded me of my brother. I think that's why I liked him so much. On a subconscious level, that must have been why I offered him Vincent's room instead of any of the other spare bedrooms.

I grabbed Art's tracksuit jacket out of the washing machine and checked it for scent of vomit, it was all clear. Out of habit, I went to make a cup of coffee for Spike but stopped myself when I remembered that Spike had been willing to leave Art outside in the street earlier to die. I decided not to take him his coffee for the first time. For some reason, having Art in the house made me feel safer than I had in a long time. Instead of making a cup of coffee, I poured

Art a glass of water and took it to him. He thanked me for the water and the jacket, both of which he placed on the bedside table, and we said goodnight. He had a funny look on his face, like he wanted to say something but wasn't sure how to say it. I assumed he was just grateful for my hospitality but didn't have the words to express himself.

Back in my room, I made Frank's day by 'finding' him under the bed and telling him that he was allowed to sleep in my room that night. Not that he was complaining, but when he asked why he didn't have to sleep on his own tonight, I explained that there was someone else sleeping in his bed for the night. This was a mistake. Frank got so excited which made it even harder to get him to sleep than usual. Frank asked who the new person was and if he could go and meet him. I explained that Art was a new friend and that he would meet him in the morning after he'd been to sleep. Frank eventually fell asleep, but I couldn't sleep that night. Something didn't feel right, and it wasn't just my new awareness of all the bugs crawling over my pillow. I had a horrible feeling that something bad was going to happen. I tried to convince myself that everything was OK, and that Art was down the hall just like my brother was when I was growing up. Vincent used to let me stay in his room if I was ever scared or if I'd had a bad dream and couldn't get back to sleep. Those memories brought me some peace and soon I was asleep.

I woke up in the dead of night to see Frank staring at me with his horrifyingly wide eyes. He'd done this in the past when he was having night terrors, but this was different. When he was having the night terrors before, it would look like he was screaming but not actually making any sound. This time he looked like he was scared and purposely trying not to make any noise. He looked me dead in the eyes and whispered:

"He's awake."

I told Frank to stay in my room while I went to check out what he was talking about. I opened the bedroom door, but couldn't hear a sound outside in the hall. Quietly, I walked towards Vincent's room where Art was staying, and noticed that the door was open. I glanced inside but couldn't see him. The glass of water I'd given him was still on the bedside table, but his tracksuit jacket was gone. If he'd got up to use the toilet in the middle of the night, why would he need to take his jacket? I crept down the stairs and checked the Den, where we'd spent most of our evening. The room was empty with the exception of my pet chameleon who hadn't made an appearance all evening but was now bathing in the last remaining embers of the fireplace. I gestured to him as if to say, 'where is he?', but all I received in return was an angry look and a glimpse of his tongue as he stuck it out at me. Rude.

I made my way through the rest of the house as quietly as possible, until eventually I arrived at the pantry. The door was open, and a faint light was emanating from within. I opened the door to see Art hunched over a bag full of food and other supplies. He looked shocked to see me.

Art slowly stood up and walked towards me. He no longer looked like the person I had spent the day with. His friendly smile had been replaced by a scowl and he looked angry and like he wanted to hurt me. "You should have stayed asleep" he snarled. I asked him what he was doing. "Surviving", he snapped. I began to say that he was welcome to stay here with me, that we could share the food and get through this together, but it was too late. Art ambled up to me with a look of pure hatred in his eyes. He pulled back his arm, readying himself to hit me. The last thing I remember was trying to say "You don't have to do this, just because the..."

I didn't manage to finish my sentence before his fist collided with my face.

I woke up the next morning with Frank hugging my chest for dear life, like a dreadful koala bear. I winced in pain as I felt the lump on the side of my head where Art had attacked me, but it was nothing compared to the pain and hurt I felt inside. I was suffering from an overwhelming sense of sadness and betrayal that I couldn't begin to fathom. It was different to anything I had ever experienced before. I think Frank can feel my sadness and his only way of comforting me is to grab hold of me tightly. I also think he was scared that I might not wake up.

I carefully peeled Frank off of me and reassured him that I was alright. One look over at the empty pantry told me that Art had not had a change of mind. He had cleared out almost everything we had left. I got up and started to inspect the house to see if there was anything else he had taken. Nothing else seemed to be missing downstairs, but I did have to do a double take when I got to the front door. I didn't notice at first, but a second glance revealed that the front door was still boarded up. How had he got out? Had he broken a window? Surely, he wouldn't have risked making that much noise. Then I noticed Art's backpack sitting on the floor beside the front door next to several bags full of food. Why would he leave all of this behind? Was he still in the house? I called out.

"Art?"

The lack of response didn't necessarily answer my query, so I cautiously continued to search the house. The next clue that I found was concerning, a pool of fresh blood on the floor next to the basement door.

Spike.

I didn't say his name out loud, but I sensed he could hear my thoughts…

INT. Basement. Morning.
Edward slowly walks down the basement staircase leaving the door open behind him. The absence of windows makes the space pitch black except for the faint light shining down from the hallway above. Edward reaches the bottom of the staircase and sees a body lying on the floor. It is Art's body. His T-shirt is splattered with blood which covers carefully selected sections of the shirt. The words **NOT** and **YET** were now hidden beneath thick red globules of blood. The only word that remains visible on there is **DEAD**. Spike walks out of the shadows and into the spotlight in his vampire form. He too is covered in blood.

Edward: What have you done?
Spike: I killed him.

Edward looks shocked by the vampire's matter of fact response. He steps closer to the body.

Edward: Why?
Spike: You know why. He was going to steal your food and leave you for dead. Artemis was a bad person Edward. Trust me. I saw it.
Edward: *(raising his voice)* No! He wasn't. He was just desperate. He didn't think he had a choice. He wasn't a bad person. I spoke to him, I got to know him. You have no idea!
Spike: I saw inside his mind, Edward. I know he was a bad person.
Edward: What do you mean you saw inside his mind?
Spike: When I drink someone's blood, I see and feel their thoughts, their feelings. Even their memories.
Edward: So what? That doesn't mean you knew him. *(Shouting)* THAT DOESN'T MEAN HE DESERVED TO DIE!
Spike: If I hadn't killed him, he would've come back here and not alone. He would have brought bad people with him, Edward. Bad people that would want to take this place for themselves.
Edward: You can't know that. And even if you did, I could have spoken to Art, I could have stopped him, explained to him… I could have saved him.

Spike: He didn't want to be saved. He was only looking out for himself. People don't change Edward. That old man who was running after him yesterday, why do you think he was chasing him?
Edward: I don't know.
Spike: Artemis killed that old man's son in cold blood. That's why the old man was chasing him; to avenge his dead son.
Edward: No. You can't know that. You're lying!
Spike: I saw it, Edward. I do not lie. You were so blinded by the idea of having your brother back, you could not see Artemis for what he truly was; a villain. He deserved to die. That's why I killed him. That's what I do. I take life away from those who do not deserve it.

Edward pauses for a moment to think.

Edward: But how? You don't have your teeth.
Spike: I don't need my fangs to kill Edward, and I don't need them to drink blood. I never did.
Edward: But mum took them so that you'd stop killing people. If you didn't need them, why did you come back here?
Spike: I had a reason to be here.

Once again Edward pauses to reflect. He delves deeper into his archives this time.

Edward: You attacked my mum. That first night. You said you only kill bad people. Then why were you attacking her? Were you trying to kill her?
Spike: No. I was trying to stop her. I told you, the lady is a good person.
Edward: Stop her from what? What was she doing?
Spike: I'm afraid I cannot explain that, Edward.
Edward: You threatened to kill me!
Spike: I was never going to harm you, Edward. You are not a bad person. I just needed you to let me stay here.
Edward: Well, I don't want you here anymore. You're a murderer and I want you out of my house!
Spike: I must stay here until the lady returns.
Edward: *(Screaming)* SHE'S NOT COMING BACK! SHE'S DEAD!

Edward hears a gasp from the top of the stairs. He turns around to see a very shocked looking Frank up at the doorway. The living voodoo doll looks mortified. Tears are rolling down his face.

Edward: Frank!

Frank scuttles away. Edward looks down and sighs.

Spike: I was just trying to protect you.

(Pause)

Edward: Art... Will he turn?
Spike: No.

Edward slowly walks up the stairs. Spike grabs Art's arm and drags his corpse back into the shadows.

Edward shuts the basement door behind him, leaving the scene in complete darkness.

Survival Rule #5 - Trust No One

Anyone outside of your bubble must be treated as an enemy. Under no circumstances should you trust an outsider.

I followed Frank up the stairs and found him on the third floor sitting beside the telescope. I asked him what he was doing, and he told me that he was looking to see if he could see mum in heaven. The inexplicable feeling of sadness and emptiness that I had woken up with somehow managed to multiply. I didn't know what to say to Frank to make him feel better. Instead of finding words, I just returned his koala bear hug and stood with him in silence for a while. I didn't want to tell Frank that I hadn't meant what I said about mum being dead. He's a very literal being, and might not understand me if I told him that I didn't mean it. And the truth is, I did mean it. It's been years since mum left. If she was coming home, she'd be back by now.

A little while later, I went back downstairs with the intention of cleaning up the blood by the basement door. I stopped when I passed the front door and saw Art's backpack again. My baseball bat was still sticking out of the bag, only now the bag was also full of food and other supplies that Art had stolen from me. I decided to go through the bag to reclaim my stolen items when I came across a few of Art's possessions. At least I assumed they were his, I guess he could have stolen them from someone else. I found the following items in his bag:

- A bag of cookies that I later found out were 'special cookies.'
- A pocket watch with a small sepia photo of a woman inside it.
- A packet of sweets, the ones he had offered me yesterday.
- A Halloween mask of a skull.
- A notebook full of little stories, drawings, and odd reflections.

These were not the possessions of an evil person. I refused to believe Spike's words about Art killing someone in cold blood for no reason. The person I met yesterday couldn't have done that. I put everything back in the bag, except the notebook. I sat down and read every word in that book. In all the stories and notes he had written, not a single word gave me an inkling that he was a bad person. I knew it was his notebook too, because he had written his name after each of the short stories. I got the impression that some of them were about himself.

One story in particular stood out to me. It was about an Orc becoming an adult. Something about it made me think that it was about Art and his brother. It seemed like Art didn't want to talk to me about his brother last night. I have transcribed Art's story and drawn a picture here so you can decide for yourself:

The Young Orc – A Story by Artemis

A young Orc sets out to begin his trials to become an Orc grown. His brother tasks him to kill a wolf, then bring its body back to be shown.

The young Orc had killed before, but only in self- defence. Never had he had to take the life of innocence.

On his reluctant hunt, the young Orc came across a young wolf cub. He battled with his conscience; should he or should he not shed blood.

Inside his head his brother's voice tells him to draw his knife. He brought down his blade and with it, he ended a life.

I put the notebook back in the backpack and placed the bag inside the cupboard under the stairs, knowing it would be kept safe by the creature that lives under there. I thought about what Art had done and what he'd been prepared to do. I felt angry, like I could never trust anyone again. I told myself that if I wanted to survive, I must never let anything like this ever happen again. But part of me also felt empathy for Art's situation. Had he really wanted to hurt me? I could never find out now.

I heard Frank shouting from upstairs. I assumed he was OK and hadn't fallen off the telescope stool, as I couldn't feel any immediate phantom pain. When I got to him, he was begging me to look through the lens of the telescope. Knowing full well I wasn't about to see a person sitting on a cloud, I decided to humour him. What I saw, and what Frank was so excited about, was a giant red hot air balloon floating through the sky not too far away. As hard as I tried I couldn't see anyone on board the balloon, but it did make me think about other people out there in the chaos of the world, as well as what Spike had said about Art's intentions to bring 'bad' people back here. Were there other survivors out there? Who was piloting that balloon?

This got me thinking about what I wanted to do next, and how much longer I could stay in this house. If there were more people out there, maybe there would be a chance for a better life somewhere else. These thoughts ended abruptly when I moved the telescope down and saw that Death was standing outside my house for the first time.

Makeup

About a year before The War started, I was in a pet shop with my mum. She would often go there to pick up animals for work. I used to ask her if I could have a pet and she would always say no, because she knew that she would end up having to look after it for me. This day was different though. After my usual circuit around the hamsters, guinea pigs and bunnies, I laid eyes on an animal I had never seen before. It was some kind of lizard. I gravitated towards the tank, as if a magnet was pulling me towards it. The sign beneath the tank said the lizard's name was 'Id' and that Id was a chameleon. Id had a tiny little body and huge eyes, almost the same size as its head, and a little curly tail. Its skin was a colour like nothing I had ever seen before. Impossibly, it was like the colour of air.

Once mum had completed her latest purchase, she and the pet shop owner wandered over to me. I asked the proprietor for more information about Id, and he told me that he'd only recently acquired the chameleon and was going to return him because he was broken. According to the pet shop owner, Id was supposed to adapt to his surroundings and change his skin colour to reflect any environmental changes around him, but he wasn't performing this miracle in the way the shop owner desired. Something about the little reptile was melting my heart, and I swear Id hadn't taken his eyes off me since I walked in.

I asked mum if we could buy him and just as she opened her mouth to decline my request as usual, the lizard shifted his independently mobile gaze from me onto her and she paused. It was as if she was listening to a voice in her head.

"We'll take him."

On the car journey home, mum told me that the chameleon was for me but that she would need to keep hold of him for some experiments first. She asked me if I wanted to change his name, but I decided not to. Something about the name Id struck me as unique and special and I liked it.

After a few days, mum told me she had something to show me regarding our new pet chameleon. When I walked into her bedroom, I noticed that Id wasn't in the little tank that we purchased from the pet shop, but instead was in a rather strange looking cage with little silver tubes sticking into it. Mum went on to casually explain to me that the chameleon wasn't broken at all, he was actually a magical force of nature that she had never seen before. She told me that she had performed one of her 'Dragon scale' experiments on him to help him reach his true potential. Then she told me that Id wasn't even really a reptile, he was actually something called an Elemental. I had no idea what she was talking about, but she had a smile on her face which meant it was a good thing. Anything that could make mum smile was a positive in my book. I never questioned the dragon scales either. I wanted to, but it was just easier not to.

Mum then explained exactly what an Elemental is in great scientific detail which sadly I haven't attempted to write down until now, but I will do my best to explain it here. Normal chameleon species can change their skin coloration to adapt to their surroundings for protection. Id doesn't change his skin colour based on his surroundings, instead his skin changes colour based on the elements of nature. This can be used as a defence as well as an offensive mechanism. There are twelve elements of nature that Id can adapt to in his own way:

I. Earth

When Id touches the dirt and rocks and soil that make up the Earth's surface, his skin turns a greenish brown colour and becomes rock solid. His tongue doubles in length to help him hunt insects. His claws also grow longer and sharper to help him dig into the ground to find worms.

II. Water

Id is able to absorb water like a sponge and expel it tenfold. If you were to put him in a bath with a small cup of water, he would be able to fill the tub in minutes. His skin turns scaly and silverish blue in colour when he is submerged in water.

III. Wind

Similar to how a bird can glide in the air, Id can summon an air current that he can ride. He's not exactly flying, more like floating, but each time I've seen him do it, he has floated higher and higher. When floating, his skin takes on a feathery appearance and turns white and brown in colour, like an eagle.

IV. Fire

This is one of Id's most powerful tools. When he is surrounded by fire, not only does he turn a bright hue of orange and red, he is also able to increase the flames in the same manner he does with water. He spends a lot of time in the chimney and the fireplace in the Den and can keep the fire burning just by being near it. I haven't had to relight the fire for years now.

V. Thunder

This element simply represents electricity. Id can manipulate electricity and is able to keep powering the backup generator, which definitely should have died by now. Whenever electricity is coursing through him, Id turns bright yellow, and you can see sparks shooting out of him.

VI. Ice

Not only can Id absorb water, but he can also control its temperature as well. He can make it so cold that it becomes ice. His skin turns an icy blue colour and he looks almost frozen himself when he does this. The room or space he is in also becomes freezing cold when he is in this form.

VII. Force

This represents the element of combat and spirit. This is the element that I have seen displayed the least. When mum was demonstrating the different elements she could manipulate, she told me that Id could move objects without touching them. I have only seen this demonstrated once because it only happens when Id is threatened, which isn't something my mum wanted to test. Once, I saw Id turn a deep purple colour when he was faced with the dead garden gnome, who seemed to be propelled backwards without being touched.

VIII. Time

This represents the past, the present and the future. Mum was particularly interested in this element, but I have never seen it demonstrated. I have no idea how to test Id for this element, or how it would manifest in him. I wonder what colour his skin would turn.

IX. Flower

Flower is representative of plants and nature. Id's presence can help things in the garden to grow just by being close by. After our first winter, a lot of the crops and vegetables were destroyed by frost. That was until Id went out into the garden. His skin turned a candy pink colour, and everything seemed to grow ten times faster when he was around. The patches in the garden where he digs for worms tend to regrow fast and more lush even when he is not around.

X. Shadow

This element represents darkness and negativity. When Id is in complete darkness, he will turn a murky shadowy green colour and his skin will glow in the dark, acting like the perfect torch. I've come to notice that this will also happen if I am in a bad mood and he's near me.

XI. Light

I would describe this as Id's standard form. This represents divinity and purity. When he is not around other elements, he is a perfectly translucent colour, almost like superglue. His skin is clear but not invisible. Mum said this could be what grants Id eternal life. She told me she thought he is well over one hundred years old and shows no signs of ageing.

XII. Moon

This represents space and the paranormal. When Id is bathed in moonlight, he turns a beautiful glowing deep blue colour. This also brings on what my mum referred to as lunar healing. If Id has an injury, it can be completely healed by exposure to moonlight. Mum once tested this on herself by inflicting a small wound on her hand and placing Id on her arm. The cut on her hand healed almost instantly. I took advantage of this special ability myself once when Frank decided that the appropriate utensil to eat an ice cream with was a butcher's knife.

I have seen Id take on one more form where his skin turns jet-black and his eyes become pure white, like they have rolled back into his head as part of some kind of trance. This happens whenever he hears me play music. He seems to really enjoy the sound of me playing guitar for some reason. The only element we haven't been able to assign a form to is Time, but I fail to see how the two are linked. If mum ever figured it out, she didn't tell me. She was understandably fascinated by the little chameleon, as am I.

Something tells me that Id has only just begun to scratch the surface of what he is capable of. He has become tremendously independent since mum left. He doesn't go into his cage at all anymore and spends almost all his time in the chimney. He seems quite happy to find his own food, but his food bowl is always available to him if he wants it.

I considered taking Id with me when I left the house to find Victoria, but I decided against it. I think that he could be an invaluable weapon out there, but I don't feel it would be fair to force the horrors of the outside world on him.

Montage

It's been a good while since I started writing this diary. I've had to put it down a few times, but I always come back to it. I've picked it up again today because I'm worried I'm starting to forget things.

I'm having trouble remembering certain chapters of my life and I'm also finding it harder to concentrate. Some memories remain clear in my mind, but others seem to be fading. I've been looking back through my archives, and it feels like some of my memories have been either edited or left on the cutting room floor entirely. So, I'm going to try harder to record more of my brother's stories and lessons. I remember he told me to never lose my imagination. He seemed to have a story for every question I ever asked him.

I once asked Vincent what it was that made all the noise inside the walls at night. He could've just told me that it was an issue with the water pressure in the pipes or something, but instead, he told me about the Goblin…

This next tale poses a question likely to give you a bit of a fright,
Have you ever wondered what's making the noise in your pipes at night?
You might think it's a house sound, but it's not,
The sound comes from a Goblin, and his name is Snot.

He rattles the pipes 'cause he wants you to know he's there,
He won't hurt you; he's not trying to give you a scare,
Snot just wants to keep you awake for as long as he can,
Broken sleep and shattered dreams are his plan.

There is no way of you silencing the sound,
Don't try to find the Goblin, he can't be found.
When you run the taps, and the water looks like ink,
It's because it's filled with Goblin waste, which really has a stink,
So be sure to check your glass before you take a drink.

Sometimes, when the hot tap is turned,
The pipes start to quiver and quake,
This is 'cause Snot is getting burned,
Now you know why your hot pipes shake,
And why your taps stick, and the hot water runs out so quick.
But you needn't worry, this Goblin won't bite,
Just accept the fact you won't get any sleep tonight.

Vincent told me that you never truly lose someone unless you lose your imagination because in your imagination, people can live forever. I try to think about him as often as I can to try to keep his spirit alive. So, I've put together a compilation of some of my favourite memories of Vincent:

- Listening to him play his guitar for hours.
- Solving the Christmas treasure hunt clues together.
- Staying up late and playing video games.
- Being introduced to movies when he showed me one of his favourite films - 'Sex, Drugs and Sausage Rolls'.
- His stories from the time he spent on the Moon.
- Watching him do his painting.
- The time he saved my life.

I know there is so much more. Some of my memories are ordinary, mundane even, while others are bizarre and hard to believe. They're just not at the forefront of my mind right now. I ask myself, am I losing my memories or starting to remember things that never really happened? Can you have memories of things that never took place?

Vincent told me that this world is created from your memories.

Continuity

As part of my recent attempt at a memory recall, I've come up against a concerning problem. Something I knew to be in this house is no longer here, and I can't work out if it is simply missing or if it never existed in the first place.

When I was little, I had a fear of the monster that lived in the cupboard under the stairs. I never actually saw the monster, but I heard my mum talking about it to her friend once. I remember she said that she used to be followed by a black monster. Wherever she went and whatever she did, she could feel the black monster following her. She said some days were good, and she would hardly see the monster at all. But other days were bad, and she would open her eyes in the morning and the black monster would be staring her in the face. As I never got to see the monster, I could only imagine what it looked like. I think this definitely made it worse. I pictured a thick black cloud of smoke with no face. It could float through walls like a ghost and disappear in an instant.

When I asked mum about this horrible monster that was following her, she told me that I wasn't supposed to know about it and that I shouldn't eavesdrop on private conversations. She told me that she was working hard to get rid of the monster, and that she'd managed to stop it from following her. She said she'd locked it in the cupboard under the stairs and was trying to stop it from getting out.

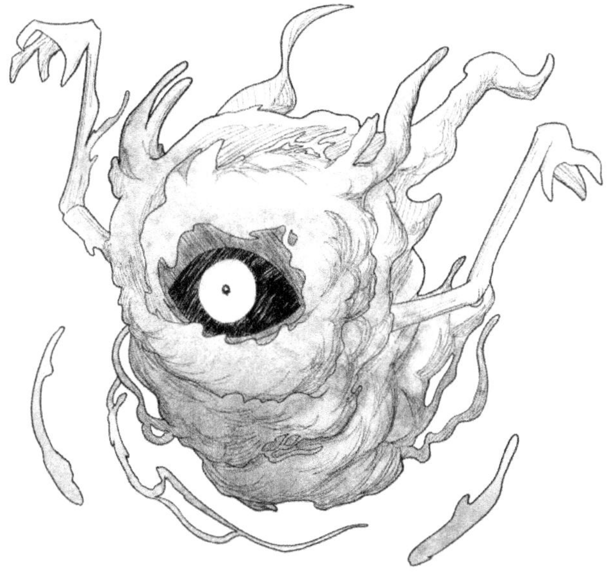

From that day on, I never went in that cupboard for fear of releasing the monster.

One day, I saw mum open the cupboard. I screamed in fear, and she quickly closed the door. It was almost as if she'd forgotten about the monster. I asked her why she'd opened the door and why she wasn't scared to let the monster out. She tried to persuade me that I didn't need to worry about the monster anymore and that she was the only person that could see it. She said the reason she was going into the cupboard was to put away some important documents and that they would be safe in there. For some reason, I didn't believe her, so that night, when everyone had gone to sleep, I crept downstairs to look inside the cupboard. I remember feeling consumed by fear, but my curiosity was too overpowering.

As I slowly opened the door, I saw a room ten times bigger than the small cupboard space I'd been expecting to see. In the middle of the room, I saw the dark, smoky figure I'd imagined in my mind. The only difference was that this monster had one giant eyeball in the centre of its face. It was deathly quiet in the cupboard, so quiet I could actually hear the creature's heart beating. The door to the cupboard creaked, alerting the monster to my presence. It flew towards me, like a hurricane.

I shut the door as quickly as I could, only to hear a loud thump as the foggy creature collided with the wood. I rushed upstairs to wake up my brother and inform him of this terrible discovery. Vincent escorted me to my bedroom and told me not to worry. He said that he would take care of it for me. Then he soothed me to sleep by telling me a story about an evil pixie who lays eggs in your ears while you're sleeping, which, in hindsight, is most likely the root cause of my earwax build up problem.

The next morning, I woke to the sound of Vincent and my mum arguing. I never found out what their quarrel was about. I also never mentioned the monster under the stairs again to either of them. Vincent said that he would take care of it, and that was enough for me. I trusted him. But I still stayed clear of the cupboard under the stairs just to be on the safe side.

Thinking back, the reason I put Art's backpack in the cupboard under the stairs was because I wanted to keep it safe, but at the same time, I didn't want to have to see it every day. I opened the door and quickly shoved it inside without looking. It only just occurred to me today how ridiculous I was being. I asked myself, what was the worst thing that could happen? I decided that I should toughen up and face my fear.

This morning, I went to the cupboard under the stairs, opened the door… and was faced with nothing. The space was so much smaller than I remembered. When I saw that there was no faceless black smoke monster in there, I decided to step inside. Other than Art's backpack, which had spilled open on the floor, the only other thing in there was a grandfather clock.

I didn't understand. Where was the monster? Had I imagined it? Had it left? Had it followed mum?

Was it ever really there? What else have I imagined?

Editing

Survival Rule #6 - Always be 100%

You must always have a plan, never attempt to make it up as you go along. Stick to the plan and don't lose your way.

I've been thinking a lot about mistakes I've made, regrets and things I wish I could've done differently. What would I do if I could go back in time? Sadly, there's no way that I know of to scroll back along a timeline and click edit on a scene you'd like to change - you can't just take a pair of scissors to a frame of film you want to cut. All you can do is work as hard as possible on today's shots so that in the future, you don't feel the need to come back and change them. I just wish so much that I would have done things differently. It goes without saying that I'd want to try and stop this apocalypse and everything that's happened because of it, but I'm also thinking about events that occurred before the end of the world...

Eyeline Match:
I would have told Victoria how I felt about her. Part of me thinks she knew, just like I know how she felt about me, even though she never expressed it verbally.

Smash Cut:
I should have paid more attention in school and made more of an effort to make friends. I shouldn't have avoided social interactions as much as I did. I had no idea how important those things would be.

Shot Reverse Shot:
I wish I'd spoken to my brother about how he was feeling. I would have told him that I cared about him and that I was there for him, always.

Match Cut:
I should've spent more time with my mum and shown more interest in her work and all the experiments. I wish I understood what she was trying to achieve.

Sound Mixing:
I wish I'd asked Vincent to teach me to play guitar properly, instead of just listening to him play all the time. It would have been good to share that with him.

Invisible Cut:
As silly as it sounds, if I could go back in time I'd make a plan for the end of the world, or at least given it some thought. If we had been better prepared, we might have been able to prevent this from ever happening or put a stop to it sooner.

Cross Dissolve:
I would have recorded more - taken more photos and videos, written down memories so they wouldn't fade away. I thought the reason I didn't do that was because I was too busy enjoying the moment, but by not recording, those memories are harder to keep in the final cut.

Rough Cut:
I would definitely have taken better care of myself, my health, and my personal hygiene…

A monstrosity lives under your bath, deep beneath the plug hole,
He's made of your hair and filth that goes down the drain,
He thrives in the deep, dark, murky, and wet terrain,
He needs all your gunk, ooze, and foulness to make him whole.

This thing is known as the Body Ogre, but we'll call him B.O,
And if you don't wash and clean at least once a week,
He will suck you through the plug hole before you can speak,
You'd better scrub yourself so clean that your skin starts to glow,
Or before you know it, you'll be pulled right down below,
Then you'll spend the rest of your days wishing that you'd bathed,
Whist being enslaved by an ogre made up of hair that you had shaved.

Score

I've been playing Vincent's guitar quite a bit recently. I find that music can really impact and magnify the overall tone and narrative of a scene. But the main reason I play is because I find it relaxing. It can act as a medium for processing my emotions, lifting my mood as well as helping me with my concentration. I find that I tend to sleep a little better at night when I've played guitar before bed. Sometimes my peace is brought to an anticlimactic end when Larry the gargoyle shouts from the roof to warn me that the Dead are close by, and that I should probably keep the noise down.

My chameleon, Id, loves to sit with me and listen while I play. He usually sits in my lap or curled up on my shoulder. As soon as the music starts, his eyes turn white, and his scales turn jet black like a note on a page of sheet music. It gives me a strange sensation, like a part of me is floating out of my body and watching the scene play out like an audience member. I am watching the moment take place up on the big screen despite being in the scene myself. It's very strange but I really enjoy it.

Today was different. I usually play guitar up on the third floor in an attempt to make less noise for the outside world, but today I decided to take the guitar into the Den to play. Id appeared from the fireplace glowing bright orange and leaving little sooty footprints on the carpet as he wandered towards me. He climbed up my leg and onto the guitar and squeezed himself beneath the strings and into the hollow sound hole. Then he curled up inside, something he's never done before.

I usually play the same piece of music; a slow melancholy composition that I call 'Edward's Theme'. For some reason, it always seems to make Frank cry when he hears it. I'm not sure why, but having Id sit inside the guitar today altered the sound that the instrument produced. I found my fingers reaching for different strings and discovering new notes. The result was a much sweeter sounding tune that simultaneously brought a smile to my face and a tear to my eye. I started to get that floating out of body feeling, but what happened next was completely different altogether.

In that moment, I wasn't looking at myself on the big screen. Instead, I saw an image of myself standing in front of Victoria. It looked like a memory I didn't own, like something that hadn't happened yet. Victoria looked older. Her hair looked messy, and her clothes well worn, but she was still as beautiful as I remembered her. I stood in front of her looking exhausted, but also the happiest I'd ever seen myself. What was this? Was it a dream? A wish? A vision of the future? How could that be possible?

Before I could analyse the scene further, I felt my fingers stop playing, the houselights came back on, and I heard the sound of the projector powering down. The scene came to an end, and I was back in my body holding a silent guitar. Alone again.

Id crawled out of the guitar. His jet-black scales already fading back to their regular translucent shade. He looked drained, like he had just been depleted of all his powers. I tried gently strumming the guitar to encourage him to come back so that I could check that he was OK, but he kept on walking towards the fireplace. He collapsed onto the burning embers and lay there for the rest of the afternoon.

I have no idea what happened earlier, but I know that it felt real. As real as those other out of body experiences.

Plot Holes

It's been so long now that I don't know if the creatures that I keep seeing running around my house are real or just in my head. This morning I saw a little yellow creature under my bed running off with one of my discarded toenails…

A little demon lives under your bed, like a set of lost car keys,
There's nothing cute about this creature, let us call her Cheese.

She eats discarded toenails that are thrown beneath the bed,
And she becomes very grouchy when she hasn't been fed.

So make sure you pick your toenails at least once a week,
Or else when you sleep, Cheese will eat them right off your feet.

I'm really starting to worry about what is real and what is in my imagination.

Is any of this real?

Is all of this in my imagination?

Am I going mad?

Have I been locked in here too long?

I think I need to go outside.

ACT V

Act V - The Twist

This is my account of the day that everything changed. Again.

The following events took place about a week after the weird out of body experience with the vision of Victoria.

The scene opens with an establishing shot of me asleep in bed.

I opened my eyes, but not to the sound of the alarm clock. The batteries had finally died, just like everything else. The time on the clock read eight o'clock as normal, but the hands were no longer ticking. For the first time in a long time, I woke up feeling good, refreshed even. It dawned on me that my reoccurring dream had been different last night. It started in a similar fashion, with the Dead breaking down the front door, but this time the dead people were all faceless; all apart from Victoria who was in the foreground of the shot. I could see her face, and she was alive. She looked just like she did in that vision I had last week. She started climbing the stairs towards me and with every step she took, the faceless dead around her started to fade away. This continued until she was standing nearly right in front of me, and there were almost no background artists left. In this version of the dream, Victoria grabbed me, but instead of pulling me down into a horde of the Dead to be ripped apart, she embraced me.

I lay in bed rubbing my eyes in an attempt to wake myself up while trying to process the meaning of the sudden change in my reoccurring dream. Could this mean that if I can somehow find Victoria, all of this will come to an end? That can't be. Victoria is dead. I saw her die.

I continued to process these thoughts as I dragged myself out of bed and got dressed for the day. The thoughts stayed with me as I walked down the hall to wake up Frank. It was only when I entered Frank's room and found his bed empty that my analysis of the dream ceased.

I knew the search for Frank would be short. Experience told me that he would be in one of four places:

* Looking for the guitar's secret hiding place.
* Searching for cookies in the pantry.
* Trying to break into mum's locked bedroom.
* Breaking his record for how long he can keep his hand in the fireplace.

As expected, it didn't take long to find him, but I was surprised when I did. As I approached the stairs, I glanced towards mum's bedroom door to see if Frank was loitering there. He wasn't, but the door was slightly ajar. As I approached the door, I noticed something on the floor outside; a small silver coin that I'd never seen before. Had Frank used this coin to somehow pick the lock on the door? I put the coin in my pocket and pushed the door open.

INT. Edward's mum's bedroom. Morning.
Edward enters the room. Light from the open curtains floods the space making it difficult to see. Amongst the empty animal cages on the floor of the bedroom, Frank's little feet protrude out from beneath the bed.

Edward: Frank?

Frank is startled by the arrival of Edward and hits his head on the bed frame as he hurriedly crawls backwards. Edward feels the blow and rubs the phantom pain on the back of his head.

Frank: Hello.
Edward: What are you doing? How did you get in here?
Frank: Mummy said, if she didn't come back, then I should give you this.

Frank drags a large wooden box out from under the bed. It is a bespoke handmade box made of oak. Its only significant detail is the silver hinge mechanism on the back, used to lift the lid. Edward steps forward to get a better look at the box that has been placed by Frank's feet.

Edward: What? How? Why are you only telling me about this now?
Frank: Because you said she isn't coming back.
Edward: I told you that ages ago. Why are you only showing me this now?
Frank: I couldn't get in. The door was locked.

Edward takes a deep breath and thinks. He makes the conscious decision not to proceed with his line of enquiry as experience tells him he will not get any satisfactory answers. Instead, he kneels down and places his hands on the box.

Edward: She wanted me to have what's inside here?

Frank: Mummy said; give the box to Edward, that it was important, and that she loved me.

Edward gives him a confused look and then quickly turns his attention to the box. He slowly opens the lid and discovers what is inside.

It has taken me a while to process what I have discovered. The following is a list of items I have found inside the box, and what I believe to be their meanings:

The Letter

The first thing I saw when I opened the box was a handwritten letter addressed to me, which I have transcribed below. This must have been what she was writing when I arrived home that day The War started, just before she left.

Dear Edward,

I am sorry for all of this. I don't have long until you return home from school. I need to get back to the lab before this gets any worse. I just need you to know that none of this was intentional. We were trying to save people, to extend human life. And selfishly, I was trying to bring Vincent back. My colleagues didn't know what I was trying to do. When the mouse's blood samples were sent to Spain, I had no idea that this would happen. I don't have time to explain more. I have to go and end this. I might be the only one left who can. Just know that I love you, and that I will do everything in my power to protect you. I'm so sorry.

All my love,

Mum

I have read and re-read this letter over and over again, and I am still in disbelief. Was she saying that she and her colleagues at the lab were responsible for this whole thing… for the end of the world? What did she mean about trying to bring Vincent back? What has Spain got to do with all of this? Is that where she is now? She said that she might be the only one that could put an end to this. Unfortunately, this damn letter has raised more questions than it has answered.

The Vials

There were two small blood vials tied together with a piece of string. One was full of blood; the other almost empty. I untied the string and looked closely at the vials. They had labels with names written on each of them. The one that was full of blood had *Edward's DNA* written on the label, and the almost empty vial read *Vincent's DNA*. These can't be the same blood samples she mentioned in the letter, because that referred to mice blood… She must have been talking about Squib.

Mum mentioned that she had used my DNA to help create Frank, but the blood vial with my name on it was still full. Did that mean she had more of my blood somewhere, and how did she even get hold of it? It was only when I started asking myself these questions that a forgotten memory came back to me, like when you watch your favourite movie, and a scene comes on that you've never seen before because your copy of the film was recorded from the TV, and that scene was cut to make time for the adverts. Or something…

I remember mum coming into my room the night before The War began. I was half asleep, but I recall her stroking my arm and suddenly feeling a sharp scratch. Was that when she took my blood? I remember stirring and her putting her hand on my forehead and telling me to go back to sleep. I'm worried that I've invented this memory and that it didn't actually happen. I don't know why she'd have a vial of Vincent's blood too.

The Envelope

The next item in the box was an envelope. It wasn't addressed to me, but it was marked with a circle and the number 1, just like the treasure hunt envelopes mum used to make for us at Christmas. She would leave clues that led to a gift, but she hadn't done this since before Vincent disappeared. I wondered whether this was the one she'd prepared for us just before Vincent left, or was this something she'd put together just for me more recently. I opened the envelope and read the clue inside. It became clear.

Edward,
This year's secret treasure hunt will only have one phase,
You can find the treasure by going lots of different ways,
It could take you minutes, hours or even days,
From now on we will call this challenge The Christmas Maze…

Reading this is giving me a headache. Envelope 1 is supposed to lead me to envelope 2, which would have a clue to where I can find number 3, and so on. This tells me nothing. I still don't know where to find the second envelope. I can't imagine the 'treasure', as she called it, could be very significant anyway.

If it was something important, surely, she would've just given it to me beforehand or left it inside the box. But the fact that she took the time to put this challenge together for me after all this time really makes me happy. I know how hard it must have been for her.

The Medication

The fourth item in the box was a small pot of tablets that had been prescribed to my brother. The name of the medication had been scratched off, but the directions on the bottle stated that the tablets should be taken twice a day, and the small print indicated that they were to help with a delusional disorder, something I didn't even know he had. I've searched the library, but I can't find any books on delusional disorders, or medications to treat them, and obviously the Internet is no longer an option. I guess that mum just kept hold of the tablets in case Vincent ever came back. I don't know why else she would've kept them in this box.

The Photo

Under the medication I found a photograph. There were four people in the photo who appeared to be standing on a sunny beach. I recognised my mum and a very young Vincent, as well as a baby who I'm guessing was me, although it's an ugly looking thing. The fourth person in the image was a man I didn't recognise. Was this my dad? They all look so happy. Vincent looks old enough in the photo to remember this being taken, yet I don't remember him ever once mentioning our dad. This clearly meant enough to mum for her to keep it here, but why has she never shown it to me before? I turned the photograph around to find an inscription that read:

El Campello.
Our first family holiday. X

I have no memory of this photo given that I was just an incredibly ugly baby when it was taken, I just can't work out the reason why it is in this box.

The Card

Behind the photograph was an old pink envelope with a card inside. This was the card that I'd given mum on the first Mother's Day after Vincent went missing. It looked tatty and worn out, like it had been handled frequently. I was worried it might fall apart when I touched it. Carefully, I opened the card and read the handwriting inside:

Please don't be sad anymore.
Love, Edward

I can't believe she kept this. I didn't realise it was so precious to her.

The Password

The next thing I found in the box was a small piece of paper with some numbers written on it:

2006

I guess this must be the password for something. Why else would she deem this piece of paper important enough to keep in this box? The numbers don't mean anything to me though.

The Key

The penultimate item in the box was a black key, the end of which was shaped like a skull. There was a chain attached to it so that someone could wear it around their neck like a necklace. This was pretty cool, but again, I don't recall ever seeing it before. I don't know what it unlocks.

The Note

This final item broke me. I've really struggled to write this down. At the bottom of the box was a small purple post-it note with black text which was difficult to read. It was from Vincent. I have never seen this before...

For my brother,
Know that it is OK to not be OK.
I'm not OK.
But that's OK.
All the love I have left,
Vincent.

I want to know why I've never seen this before and why mum kept it from me. Did she show it to me, but I've forgotten? Could I have blocked it from my memory because it was too painful? Was she trying to protect me? Did Vincent write this for me before he left? The questions racing through my mind are torturing me.

When I read the note for the first time, Frank felt the need to come and hug me, like when pets have a sixth sense and somehow know when you're sad. He held on to me for a while, and I let him. It took me some time to compose myself.

An uncomfortable amount of mystery shrouds these items which I'm struggling to deal with. I need answers but I don't know how to find them. The only person that could reveal more about mum's letter would be mum herself. The blood vials are interesting though. It took me a while, but I eventually remembered what Spike had told me - that when he drinks people's blood, he can feel their memories. I wondered what he'd be able to tell me if he tasted the last few drops of Vincent's blood. Maybe Spike would be able to feel what Vincent was thinking the day he left. Maybe he could explain why he left. I wonder if he could tell me where Vincent is now?

I detached myself from Frank's koala grip, put the black skull key around my neck, and raced down to the basement as fast as I could.

The basement door was ajar. I hadn't been anywhere near the door since Spike had murdered Art. I haven't forgiven the vampire for that, but I need his help. This doesn't mean I'm going to start making him cups of coffee every night again. As far as I'm concerned, any relationship we may have had is dead. I'm not stubborn enough to pretend I don't need his help though. It's the least he can do for me.

The basement was flooded in its usual ocean of darkness, and I couldn't see a thing. I made my way to the bottom of the staircase and called out the vampire's name.

"Spike!"

No response came from the darkness. I edged further into the giant basement and called out again. The silence was ear-shattering. My cautious voice echoed off the walls and bounced back at me like a stranger's whisper in my ear. Although I couldn't see or hear Spike, I got the strange feeling that I wasn't alone down there. Someone was watching me, but I couldn't see who. The only thing I could glimpse in the darkness was a faint green glow coming from the depths of the basement's void. I attempted to creep towards the light. Not being able to see where I was putting my feet made me feel as though I was about to blindly walk off the edge of a cliff. Knowing this was impossible, even for this house, I pressed on. My curiosity was enough to guide me towards that little green light, but I knew it wasn't going to be Spike. I had to find out what it was though.

I must have been walking for about a minute by this point - it's crazy how big this space is. Then, suddenly, I saw it. In the furthest corner of the basement, I found the source of the faint green light that had bewitched me.

It was Id, the chameleon. He'd made it all the way down here and because of the absolute absence of light, he was glowing in the dark.

I asked him what he was doing down here, knowing I wasn't going to get an answer. He looked me in the eyes and then glanced down at what it was he was perching on top of. It was a giant green egg. I appreciate that I ask a lot of rhetorical questions on these pages, but honestly, what the hell is this now?

I put the blood vial back in my pocket, accepting that this mission had been postponed for now. I approached Id and stuck out my hand for him to jump on, which he did. He wrapped his long tail around my wrist and clutched my fist, forming a makeshift torchlight on the end of my arm. I shone the light at the egg in an attempt to get a closer look. It was dark green in colour and about the size of a watermelon. There was no way that this egg could belong to Id and as far as I'm aware, vampires don't lay eggs either. So, how did it get here?

Exhausted by the questions swirling around my head, I turned around and made my way back to the staircase, with the helpful use of Id as a torchlight. I had enough going on to have to now worry about the sudden existence of a strange giant egg in my basement as well. On my return journey, I noticed something that I hadn't seen when I had entered the basement. A message written on the wall in what I can only assume was blood.

I'Ve gOne to fInD hER

The blood wasn't dripping wet, but it wasn't quite dry either. I don't think the message had been here very long.

A routine check of the boarded-up doors and windows upstairs told me that the only way Spike could have left the house was through the third story window last night. Last night, while I was dreaming.

Is this another sign that I should leave this house? Yet another question I don't have an answer for.

I decided that the best way to process all of this information was to go back to bed. I went to the bathroom and discovered that I had finally run out of my lifetime supply of cotton buds for my ears. If that isn't a sign that I need to leave the house, I don't know what is.

Ghosting

Today was probably the most disturbing day I've had for years. Frank told me he could hear something strange and that the noise was coming from the attic. This in itself wasn't anything out of the ordinary; there's always something scuttling around in this house making creepy noises. Today was different though.

We went up to the attic to investigate. I couldn't see anything, but when I turned around to speak to Frank, he was frozen stiff with terror. Again, this wasn't a red flag as Frank has a history of overreacting to things. I remember the first time he saw me pull a carrot out of the ground; he didn't speak for a week. It was great. But his reaction in the attic was something I hadn't seen before.

When I asked him what was wrong, he simply pointed behind me. I turned around, but there was nothing there. Frank just kept on pointing, his mouth hanging wide open. I reassured him there wasn't anything there.

Finally, he spoke.

"Ghost."

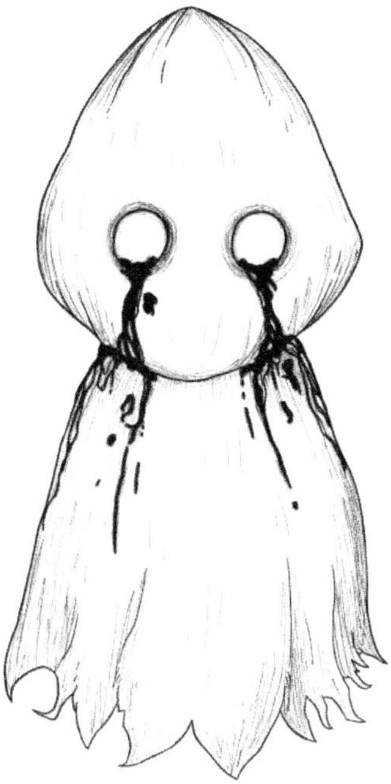

Frank claims there is a ghost in the attic, but I can't see it. He said the ghost was crying. Now, Frank might not be the smartest spoon in the drawer, but one thing he's not is a liar. He's incapable of telling lies, he doesn't know how. The fact that there is a ghost in my attic isn't what worries me, it's the fact that I can't see or hear it.

I asked Frank what the ghost was doing, but he didn't respond. We were up there for a while, but Frank didn't give me any other information until we left. When we came down, Frank told me that the ghost was speaking to him. He said that the ghost kept repeating the same word over and over and over…

“Leave.”

I asked Frank to come back up to the attic with me to see if we could communicate with it further, but he started screaming. I’ve never seen anything like it. I mean I’ve heard Frank scream before, like the time he stuck a dessert fork in the plug socket... But this was different. He seemed genuinely terrified. I could feel it in my heart.

I won’t make him go back up there. But I just can’t stop thinking about it. I can’t help wonder who it might be up there and why they want us to leave, and why Frank is so frightened.

This feels like another clear sign telling me to leave this house. They seem to be stacking up thick and fast at the moment.

Props

I've made up my mind. I'm going to go. I don't know when, but I'm going. I have to.

My plan is to try to get to mum's laboratory. It's the only place I'm going to be able to get some answers. It must be where she is, and more than likely, it will be where Spike has gone to look for her. The lab isn't that far away. Mum always said it was a 40-minute walk but if she power walked, she could make it there in 39 minutes. I'm certain that I can make it there and back in a day, which means I won't have to worry about leaving Frank on his own for too long.

Survival Rule #7 - Defence Is Key

You should never attack the Dead but should always be ready to defend yourself. Your weapon must always be kept close.

I've been trying to decide what to take with me on my journey. I won't be gone for long, so I'm hoping I won't need much.

Art's backpack - I lost my backpack the last time I ventured outside, so I'm going to take Art's.

The black steel baseball bat - It feels strange to reclaim this, but it's the only real weapon I have.

The black skull key - I've been trying to find out what it unlocks ever since I found it in that secret box that mum left me. I still don't know what it's for, but I think there is a chance that I will find out at the lab.

Food - There's a chance I'll face complications out there. I could get stuck somewhere for a while and I might need food. I'm going to leave as much as I can in the pantry for when I come back.

The blood vial - If I can find Spike, I want him to drink what's left of Vincent's blood so that he can tell me what happened to him.

A map - Although I'm pretty sure I know the way, I've never actually walked there before.

I'm honestly terrified about what might happen to me when I leave, but I know that I can't just give up and stay in this house forever. There's a strong chance that I won't make it there and back again. So, if this journey is to be my last, there are some things I need to do before I leave.

END
CREDITS

End Credits

Despite all the signs indicating that it's time to leave, I haven't been able to bring myself to go just yet. It's like there's something keeping me here. Fear, probably. That's all. There's no magical force keeping me locked inside these walls. If anything, it feels like the opposite - like something is trying to force me to leave. The problem is that each time I've opened the front door since The War started, someone has ended up dead.

There are a lot of reasons to leave. I have to find out what happened to my mum. I need to find Spike so that he can hopefully tell me what happened to Vincent. I need to find out what my dream about Victoria meant and if she really is dead. There are so many questions that need answers and the only way I'm going to get them is by leaving this house. Although, I don't think I can leave now. Not until I solve this Christmas maze riddle that mum left me anyway.

It's just impossible. No matter how much I try, no matter how many times I read it, I just can't solve it.

Can you?

INT. Kitchen. Late afternoon.
Edward is holding onto the Christmas maze envelope marked with the number 1. He opens it and shows the content to Frank.

Frank: Who, me?
Edward: Yes, you. Who else would I be talking to?

Frank leans forward to read the clue. The stitches holding his button eye in place start to come loose, which makes Edward feel a bit sick.

Frank: I don't want to go out there.
Edward: Where?
Frank: The secret garden.

Of course! The maze at the back of the secret garden. I'd forgotten all about it. It's so obvious when I read it now. But how did Frank solve it so quickly? He still struggles to drink juice out of a cup without hitting himself in the eye with it, but he was able to solve this riddle in seconds. Rather than questioning Frank's abilities and confusing the situation further, I decided to head out to the garden. Frank didn't follow me outside as he is still very much afraid of the dead garden gnome who I'm sure I will run into on my search for the treasure.

Outside was oddly quiet. The dead gnome was nowhere to be seen, so I made my way to the back of the garden. The entrance to the secret garden was wildly overgrown as no one had been through it in years. I was just a small boy the last time I went back there, accompanied by Vincent on big brother duty.

I pulled down a few vines to clear a path to the entrance of the maze. Normally things from your childhood seem smaller when you grow up, but for some reason the maze looked so much bigger than I remembered. It was as if the hedges that formed the maze had turned into thick brick walls. Upon entering, I was immediately given a choice of turning left or right. To the left was a golden hour sunset on the horizon, beautifully colourful flowers and a faint glimpse of a steppingstone path beneath the overgrown grass underfoot. To the right was a poorly lit corridor of weeds and nettles with no discernable pathway amongst the sharp stones and mud. Before I could give the decision too much thought, the choice was made for me as the sun-kissed horizon to the left became occupied by the sound of a very small, but very angry, zombie garden gnome. I knew he'd make an appearance at some point. I guess it was good to get it out of the way early.

As he ran at my ankles for the hundredth time, completely oblivious to the pain he was about to suffer, I felt almost sorry for him. My foot connected squarely with the centre of his little terracotta face, sending him flying all the way back down the path, scored by a faint squeal like that of a baby pig. Rather than facing him again and finding out if there were any more of his kind lurking in the shadows, I decided to turn right.

The dark and dreary path I'd chosen seemed to go on forever. I couldn't understand how all of this had managed to fit inside the back of our garden. It was like a forest. Eventually, I turned a corner and came to another crossroads where another choice had to be made. This time, both options looked as bad as each other. As I took a moment to analyse my options, I began hearing whispers coming from the bushes behind me.

"Where's he going?"

I turned and tried to look for where the voices were coming from but could see nothing in front of me. I made my choice and moved on through the maze. As I continued down my chosen path, the whispers got louder.

"He's not going to find it."

I thought I could see strange little faces peeping through the bushes at me, but every double take was met with disappointment.

As I approached my third optional route of the maze, I thought I saw the dead garden gnome again in the distance. I'd chosen the path that he wasn't occupying though. I was concerned with how he had managed to get ahead of me. Was there another path he had taken, or was there another gnome? I soon got my answer.

"Should we stop him?"

I quickened my pace. The creepy peeping faces in the bushes seemed to be getting more and more obvious. A lot of them were easy to see now as they were poking their faces further out from the ivy clad walls. The faces belonged to members of the missing army of garden gnomes. So, this is where they've been hiding. Every corner I turned revealed more and more to me. I started to see tiny little pairs of shoes sticking out from the bottom of the trees, small red hats poking over the tops of the walls, and the sound of pocket-sized pottery footsteps seemed to be following me around every bend.

Just as I was about to really panic about the situation, I turned a corner and stepped into a big open space.

"He's here!"

The impossibly large open area was surrounded by four giant hedge walls that were decorated with hundreds of black and white flowers. There didn't appear to be another entrance to this space. The only way in or out of this place was through the makeshift doorway that I was standing in. The centre of the open space was occupied by what appeared to be a large cage made from wooden twigs and sticks and bits of moss. Creepy. There was a rickety doorway to the cage that looked like it was about to fall over. Most intriguingly was the giant mushroom standing next to the cage. I've never seen a mushroom that big before. How had it managed to grow to that size? I wondered whether Id had been back here.

"Is he here to help us?"

I approached the cage cautiously. All of a sudden, a small garden gnome appeared on top of the giant mushroom and looked down at me. His little hat was pulled down over his eyes, but I could tell that he was looking at me with the same expressionless look that the gnome in the drinks cabinet gives me. This garden gnome wasn't like the dead one I had faced in the maze; this one was very much alive.

EXT. The Secret Garden. Late afternoon.
Edward stands by the giant mushroom gazing down at the garden gnome. The gnome raises his little staff in the air and begins to speak in a deep and booming voice. Deep and booming for a 6-inch novelty garden ornament anyway.

The Quest Wizard: *Greetings traveller! Congratulations on making it this far into the maze. Allow me to introduce myself. I am The Quest Wizard.*
Edward: (Pause) Hello?
The Quest Wizard: *Well met young sir. It is my duty to inform you that your quest through this maze has not yet reached its climax. Your quest has only just begun, dear boy.*

Edward turns around to see at least thirty more gnomes standing behind him, staring with eager anticipation. They are hiding no longer.

The Quest Wizard: *What awaits you, Outsider, are the gruelling Gnome Trials. In order to proceed and reach the treasure at the very heart of the maze, you must complete these wretched trials. Each challenge will be more difficult than the last. They are all designed to test your heart, your strength, and your will. Only the worthiest of heroes can succeed and be granted access through the final doorway. Danger awaits only the bravest soul who dares to take on these trials, young one. Only the most intelligent warrior can solve my riddles. And only the chosen one shall complete the quest and achieve eternal glory. Do you dare to begin?*

Edward pauses. He looks at the flimsy wooden door blocking his pathway to the treasure.

Edward: What happens if I just walk past you without solving your riddles?

The Quest Wizard looks baffled. His booming voice shrinks.

The Quest Wizard: *What?*
Edward: The door isn't locked. What happens if I just walk through it?
The Quest Wizard: *Well… Well that would just be poor quest etiquette.*
Edward: OK. I think I'm just going to go straight in. I'm in a bit of a rush.
The Quest Wizard: *Oh… I see. Very well.*

The Quest Wizard, looking completely dejected. He watches as Edward easily opens the flimsy wooden door and walks inside.

Well, that was easy. I entered the wooden cage feeling a little guilty though. I felt bad for the little quest gnome. He'd probably been waiting for years to deliver that speech. Maybe I'll come back one day and go through his trials to cheer him up.

My focus shifted away from the gnome quite quickly when I saw what was inside the cage. There was what looked like a mysterious open well at the back. Goodness knows where that leads to. Exploring further, I could also see a stone plinth in the middle of the cage with a small wooden box perched on top of it. The box looked remarkably similar to the one I found in mum's room. Almost as if the boxes were a pair, with the smaller one being able to fit perfectly inside the larger one, like Russian dolls.

I approached the plinth and carefully opened the little box. Inside was an envelope with a star drawn on it, just like the ones we would find at the end of our Christmas treasure hunts. I opened the envelope and pulled out a note, which read:

This must be kept secret,

For this is the last of the Dragon scales,

This must be kept safe,

Only to be used when all hope fails...

Under the envelope was a small black velvet drawstring bag. I opened the bag and emptied its contents. All that was inside was a dark green scale. No further instructions or useful bits of information. But the longer I held the scale in my hand, the heavier it felt, and I could've sworn that it started to heat up in my palm. It even looked like it was starting to glow. I quickly placed it back in its bag.

Did this mean that mum's stories of Crispy the Dragon were real? Were her theories about bringing these creatures to life using dragon scales actually true?

There really was a dragon in the basement.

CGI

My reasons not to leave this house are running out. I have been battling with myself all week in an attempt to gain that final push I need to walk out of the front door. My bag is packed, my goal is set. I thought I was ready to go yesterday. That was until my unexplainable incident with the bathroom mirror.

INT. The Bathroom. Night.
Edward has woken in the middle of the night to use the toilet. He enters the bathroom and turns on the light. He stares at himself in the mirror. His reflection stares back at him angrily. The face in the mirror begins to speak.

Mirror: WHAT ARE YOU DOING?
Edward: I don't know anymore.
Mirror: YOU CANNOT LEAVE THIS HOUSE.
Edward: Why not?
Mirror: BECAUSE YOU WILL FAIL. JUST LIKE YOU FAILED VICTORIA.
Edward: But, my dream. In my dream she was alive.
Mirror: SHE'S DEAD. JUST LIKE EVERYONE ELSE YOU'VE EVER CARED ABOUT.
Edward: I don't know that, not for certain. I have to try to find out the truth.
Mirror: AND THEN WHAT? WHAT WILL HAPPEN TO FRANK? WILL YOU LEAVE HIM HERE ALONE, WILL YOU LET HIM DIE TOO?
Edward: No, I'll come back for Frank. I'll look after him, like I always have. I'll always protect him.
Mirror: NO YOU WON'T. DON'T YOU UNDERSTAND? AS SOON AS YOU LEAVE THIS HOUSE, YOU WILL BE KILLED. YOU ARE WEAK. YOU ARE PATHETIC. YOU CANNOT PROTECT ANYONE. NOT EVEN YOURSELF.
Edward: I'm trying my best. I'm doing everything I can.

The face in the mirror flashes like a frame jump in a film reel. It is no longer Edward's face reflecting back at him. Instead, Art's blood splattered face glares back at him.

Art: I TOLD YOU EDWARD, THE WORLD IS DEAD, WE'RE JUST LIVING IN IT.
Edward: No. I don't believe that. I won't believe it.

The image in the mirror jumps again. Victoria's ghostly pale face reflects back at Edward. The word 'LEAVE' written in thick, sticky blood appears on the wall behind him.

Victoria: YOU KILLED ME, EDWARD. IT'S ALL YOUR FAULT! WHY DID YOU LET ME DIE?
Edward: I was trying to save you. I'm sorry.

The mirror flashes to the sound of a thunderclap. We see a quick shot of the pumpkin faced scarecrow before Edward's own reflection finally returns. The writing on the walls has multiplied. The word 'LEAVE' is now scrawled across every inch of the room.

Mirror: YOU ARE A COWARD. YOUR MOTHER WOULD BE ASHAMED OF YOU.
Edward: Stop it.
Mirror: IT IS OVER. YOU CANNOT WIN. YOU ARE NOTHING. GIVE UP NOW OR YOU WILL DIE.
Edward: (Screams) Shut up!

Edward punches the mirror, cracking the glass and cutting his hand. Dark crimson blood drips slowly into the sink.

Edward stares back at his true reflection in the shattered mirror. He sees his true self for the first time. The writing on the walls behind him has disappeared.

I will not listen to this. These dark thoughts that have been buried in my mind are trying to play tricks on me, and I won't let them. I am in control of my own life. I make my own decisions. I know what I have to do.

It's time. I'm finally ready.

Extreme Long Shot

Before I leave, I want to record one last memory, just in case I don't come back.

As this is to be my last night in the house for I don't know how long, I decided to play guitar for Id one last time. I thought it would be nice to play in Vincent's room. Frank sat next to me on Vincent's bed. He doesn't usually like listening to me play as it makes him sad, but for some reason he decided to join me tonight. I haven't told him about my plan to leave yet, and to be honest, I don't know how to tell him. I think he can sense that something is wrong though.

Id curled up on my shoulder and I started to play.

After playing my usual piece of music for a few minutes, Id crawled inside the guitar like he did before. The notes flowing from the guitar suddenly became softer and I started to float outside of my body again. I looked down at the two of us sitting on the bed. Only, it wasn't Frank and I sitting side by side, it was me and Vincent. Another partially deleted scene from my archive began to play out in front of me.

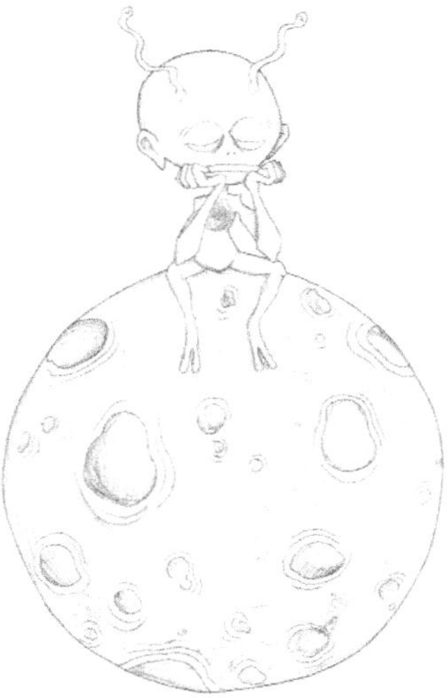

The scene took place soon after Vincent returned home after the first time he ran away. He was telling me all about how he had boarded a ship and flown to the moon, and that's why he couldn't call us to tell us where he was. He told me he'd been there for a couple of weeks, and that he'd met a little alien named Spiral.

Spiral the alien lives alone on the dark side of the moon,
He has a small spiral on his chest and a head like a balloon.

He always felt misunderstood and became very isolated.
The people around him made him feel worthless, sad, and hated.

He felt different to all the friends and family he had known,
And that things might be better if he could just live alone.

Vincent told me that he had spoken with the alien for a while, and it made him feel better. He told Spiral that it might help him if he spoke to his friends and family and told them how he was feeling. He said he knew that talking about his feelings might not be easy, but it was important to realise that he wasn't alone.

Looking down at this scene, I could see the tears in my brother's eyes. The sound of mum's voice came from downstairs – she was calling to us. Vincent told me to go and find out what she wanted, so I ran off, but he stayed behind. The non-diegetic sound of the guitar was starting to fade, but the scene continued. Vincent stood up and walked over to his desk. He picked up a black pen and a purple post-it note. I could see the message he had written:

For Mum,

I will live my life for you.

Love,

Vincent.

He put the note in what appeared to be a secret compartment concealed inside his desk drawer and then exited the room. The scene ended.

The music stopped, and I was suddenly back in my body again. Frank was sitting next to me, a single tear in his eye. Id crawled out of the guitar and clambered back up onto my shoulder. I stood up and walked over to the desk. I opened the drawer and lifted up the false bottom to reveal the secret compartment that I never knew existed until now. The note was still there. He never gave it to her.

Epilogue

Survival Rule #8 - Keep going

No matter how tough things become, you have to pick yourself up and keep going. It's one of those unwritten rules that someone really should write down.

Art was wrong. The world hasn't ended. It's not dead, not yet anyway. Not while I'm still here. What I was trying to say to Art before he knocked me out cold, was that just because the world feels like a bad place to you right now, that doesn't mean you should make it any worse.

I'm finally ready to begin my quest. I'm leaving today, so this will be my last entry until I return, and I thought that this entry should be about Frank, my strange little voodoo doll companion.

I've been putting off having the conversation with him where I finally tell him about my plan to leave the house. I have struggled to find the right words to express my reasons for leaving to him. I know that if everything goes to plan, I could get to the lab and back before he even notices I've gone. But if there are complications, there is a chance that I could be gone for a long time, with no way of knowing when I'll be back. There's also the chance that I may never return at all.

I underestimated how difficult telling Frank would be. I think it was one of the hardest conversations I've ever had.

INT. The Living Room. Morning.
Edward is trying to explain to a very confused Frank why he is leaving the house today.

Frank: I don't understand.
Edward: I have to go out there to find some answers. I need to find out what mum was doing at the lab and why she left us. I have to try and find her.
Frank: You said she died.
Edward: I know. I'm sorry I said that, but the truth is, I don't really know what happened to her.
Frank: I can come with you?
Edward: No, it's too dangerous. I need you to stay here and look after the house. I need you to stay safe.
Frank: She told me to look after you.

Edward: I know she did. And you have looked after me. You've kept me sane and given me purpose. You've been there for me this whole time. I'm not going to be gone long. I am coming back.
Frank: That's what mummy told me before she left.
Edward: I promise you. I will come back for you.

(Pause)

Frank: Please don't go.
Edward: I'm sorry. I have to. I'm so sorry. But I need to find out what happened to her. If there is a way to end all of this, I have to find out.

Frank starts to cry.

Frank: Please don't leave me.
Edward: I'm not leaving you. I will never leave you. You are a part of me. You always will be.

Edward embraces Frank.

I feel incredibly guilty for leaving him behind, but I know it is the only way. I'm doing this for him, and I'm doing this for me. I want to be able to take him outside and give him a normal life. I want to be able to take him to the seaside one day and let him create some real memories.

I know in my heart that I will return to this house. I need to. I will do everything in my power to make my way back home.

I know what it is I'm searching for. Hope.

We close on a wide shot of a beautiful old gothic mansion bathed in early morning sunlight. Our hero exits the property wearing a red backpack with a black steel baseball bat sticking out of the zipper, and a black skull key on a chain around his neck. He turns back to wave goodbye to the plump little pillowcase with horrifying eyes. The door closes, and he steps away.

The last thing we see is our hero gently placing a small black velvet drawstring bag into his pocket.

Fade to black.

The End.

Post-Credits Scene

I don't have much time.

Like in so many great movies, the main action will have to take place off screen, as I don't have the time to record it here.

My mission did not go well. I have been injured. I've returned home to assess the damage. It's not good.

I can't stay here. I can't put Frank at risk.

If social media were still a thing, I'd have a great post for today. As it doesn't exist anymore, I'll leave my final message here…

Just been bitten by a zombie. FML.

SPECIAL
FEATURES

Disclaimer

Those who do not wish to have the fourth wall torn down need not read any further.
- The Quest Wizard

The Making Of

These are some early concepts from back when the book was in the development stage.

It all started with Edward and his best friend Frank, the living voodoo doll. Some of the original ideas for the story were conceived as far back as 2006. Early plans were to create a comic book instead of a diary.

"Cute but horrifying"

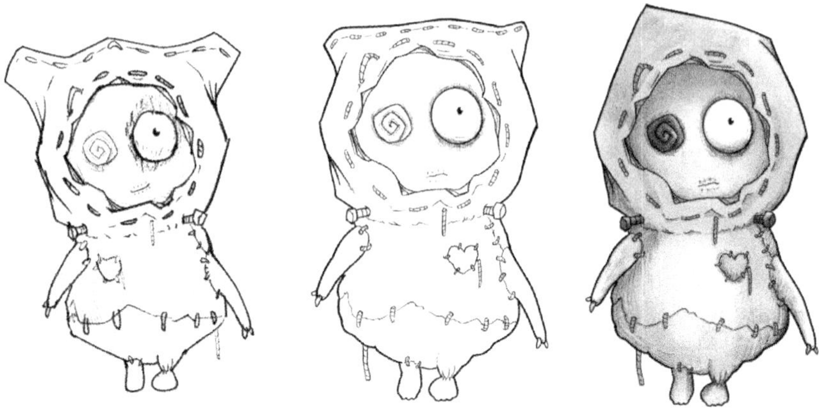

Frank The Living Voodoo Doll

The idea behind Frank's design was that he should look like a friendly little puppy but at the same time, like something that would scare the life out of you if you were to see him standing at the bottom of your bed in the middle of the night.

Frank has always felt like the heart and soul of this story.

Before the story, there were only creatures. Little drawings with a few rhyming lines describing the creations. Some of the oldest ones that have survived include Spike, the vampire with no teeth and Spiral, the alien who lives alone on the dark side of the moon.

After years of deliberating on how to bring these stories together, a decision was finally made to have Edward tell the story himself through his diary entries.

Soundtrack

Edward's Theme

This is sheet music to be played on acoustic guitar.

Movie Trivia

There is an important character in this story who is never actually named. To find out this elusive character's name, you will need to put your movie trivia knowledge to the test. Write your answers to the questions in the boxes below…

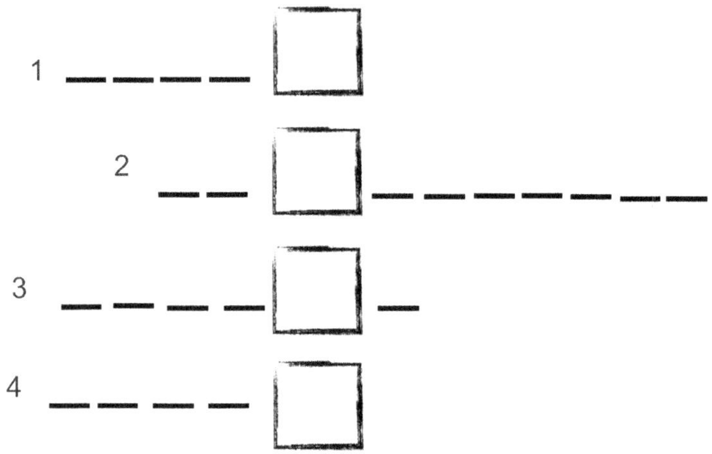

1. What is the name of the creature who throws up all over your clothes after getting dizzy in the washing machine?

2. What is the name of the creature who kicks your teeth out in the middle of the night?

3. What is the name of the overweight agoraphobic dragon who lived in Edward's basement?

4. What is the name of the fangless vampire?

If you have solved this puzzle correctly,
You will have revealed the name of Edward's mother.

Behind The Scenes

@readedwardsdiary

Follow Edward's Diary on Facebook for news, updates, competitions, and to be the first to be notified about upcoming publications and merchandise. Use the hashtag across all social media to share your thoughts on the series.

#ReadEdwardsDiary

Marketing

Welcome To

THE DEAD CLUB

Visit:

edwards-diary.myspreadshop.co.uk

Teaser Trailer

EDWARD'S DIARY

VOLUME II

Edward will return

Printed in Great Britain
by Amazon

20600690R00120